Secrets of a Victorian Household

One family. Four unexpected romances!

The Fairclough Foundation, situated in the backstreets of Westminster in London, has become a vital safe haven for women down on their luck. At the helm is resilient widow Lilian Fairclough. But now Lilian and her two daughters, Millie and Lottie, find themselves in trouble, having not heard from Millie's twin brother, Silas, for over six months…

With their dwindling funds threatening the foundation, their urgency to find out where exactly Silas is is greater than ever. And as they fight to save their livelihood, each family member is about to uncover scandalous, dangerous secrets…and find unexpected romances along the way!

Discover more in

Miss Lottie's Christmas Protector
by Sophia James
November 2019

Miss Amelia's Mistletoe Marquess
by Jenni Fletcher
December 2019

Mr. Fairclough's Inherited Bride
by Georgie Lee
January 2020

Lilian and the Irresistible Duke
by Virginia Heath
February 2020

Author Note

When I was asked if I would like to be part of this quartet I immediately said yes. It has been such fun to work with other authors crafting a story from an outline together.

The setting of this story is the Fairclough Foundation, situated in the backstreets of Westminster in 1842. It was a place of salvation for many poverty-stricken women needing shelter in the Victorian era.

Kindness, charity, inclusiveness and honesty are the overarching themes of the stories, and I can't wait to read the further adventures of Amelia, Silas and Lilian Fairclough that follow my story, *Miss Lottie's Christmas Protector*.

Merry Christmas, everyone. It's the season of giving and hope, and that's exactly what these books are all about.

SOPHIA JAMES

Miss Lottie's Christmas Protector

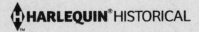

Special thanks and acknowledgment are given to Sophia James for her contribution to the Secrets of a Victorian Household series.

ISBN-13: 978-1-335-63546-4

Miss Lottie's Christmas Protector

Copyright © 2019 by Harlequin Books S.A.

Recycling programs for this product may not exist in your area.

Printed in U.S.A.

Sophia James lives in Chelsea Bay on the North Shore of Auckland, New Zealand, with her husband, who is an artist. She has a degree in English and history from Auckland University and believes her love of writing was formed by reading Georgette Heyer on vacations at her grandmother's house. Sophia enjoys getting feedback at Facebook.com/sophiajamesauthor.

Visit the Author Profile page
at Harlequin.com for more titles.

Thank you to Jenni Fletcher, Georgie Lee and Virginia Heath for making this series such an easy and fun one to write together. You were all generous with your replies and accommodating of any changes.

Prologue

In the shadow of Westminster Abbey lay an area known as the Irish Rookery—a place of narrow streets, rundown buildings and hopelessness.

This area, once a sanctuary offered to debtors and criminals by the monks from the abbey, was by 1842 the haunt of the displaced Irish, who lived in a festering labyrinth of dark and impenetrable streets full of desperation and vice.

However, social philanthropy and charity-based movements were on the rise in Victorian England, as Christian duty encouraged acts to save the souls of those mired in poverty.

The Fairclough Foundation was one such organisation and it lay in Howick Place, just on the edge of Old Pye Street, the Perkins Rents, Great Peter's Road and St Anne's Street—home to some of the worst slums in all of London.

Chapter One

Late November 1842—Westminster, London

Gilbert Griffiths, a man who was scared of his own shadow, had offered for her sister.

These words echoed through Lottie in sheer horror and growing apprehension. If Amelia accepted the overzealous and pedantic curate as a husband she would shrivel, piece by little piece, until nothing of joy and hope were left.

Charlotte Lilian Alexandra Fairclough could see the same guarded truth in Millie's eyes and she shook her head hard, unleashing wild brown curls in the process.

'You cannot love him, Millie? He is fussy and boring and impossible.'

Amelia smiled in the way that was purely her own, dutiful yet strained, a happy expression plastered steadfastly over conflict. 'He has a modest income as well as a small property and would be able to keep the wolf from our door. Did you think of that?'

'So you would sacrifice yourself for the greater good? Your life? Your for ever? There has to be a time when your selflessness has a limit, Millie. This is that time. I cannot let you do it. Not for me or for Mama.'

Her sister dug her heels in further. 'You cannot stop me, Lottie, and if I wait much longer we will all be thrown out of our house into penury. If that happens, you would be begging for me to marry him.'

'I never would. We can sell the furniture and go north. There must be enough to start elsewhere if we are frugal and besides we have…skills.'

'What skills?'

'I can sew. You can do bookkeeping and Mama can manage the rest. If we are lucky, someone far better might come along and offer for one of us and then…' She petered out. No eligible suitor had presented themselves in years. It was a groundless hope.

'And what of the vulnerable and desperate women in the Rookery who depend upon us here at the Fairclough Foundation? What would happen to them should I simply be selfish and refuse an offer of marriage that is not completely repulsive to me?'

'If it isn't, then it should be.' Lottie backtracked when she saw her sister's hurt and understood her worry about those they helped. 'Well, at least promise me that you will wait until we have a letter from Silas, telling us of all the riches he has made in America.'

The mention of their brother's absence brought a bruising sadness to Amelia's green eyes.

'He is lost, Lottie. I cannot feel him.'

As twins Amelia and Silas had always been close,

so close that Lottie had felt the odd one out in the family, the twins' sense of knowing where and how the other was was the bane of her early childhood. They had won every game of marbles, and hoop and stick, and hide-and-go-seek, the language they'd invented between them shutting her out. Often she had come across them whispering secrets and the feeling of being alone and unwanted had soon led her into trouble.

Charlotte Fairclough, the rebellious, opinionated and impulsive younger sister. The one who did not quite fit into the family structure of good deeds, fine thoughts and parsimonious self-sacrificing. Mama and Papa, Millie and Silas. In the pairings around her Lottie had had difficulty finding her place.

'I think Silas is on his way home to England even as we speak. I think he wants to surprise us.' She tried to place assurance into her words though at this moment she was feeling far from such faith.

'I think you have an imagination that is over-fertile and impossibly optimistic, Lottie, but then I suppose you always did.'

Mama chose that moment to bundle into the room, her arms full of fabric and her dark wavy hair coming a little loose from the pins that held up the thickness of it. 'I have just found this in one of the trunks your father brought from his family house years ago. I had forgotten about it completely, but it shall be perfect for us to make gowns with for Lady Alexandra's party in a fortnight.' Her eyes were wide with delight and

Lottie thought for the thousandth time how beautiful her mother was even at the grand old age of forty-five.

But then Lottie's heart fell. Lady Alexandra Malverly was her father's cousin and both the daughter of a duke and the wife of a viscount. Many of the guests at the Christmas party would be well off and odious and they would also have a keen sense of the Fairclough family's lower social standing.

Likely sensing the disenchantment in her daughters, her mother carried on.

'I know you are not as thrilled about the invitation as I am, but it is important for us to make an effort, for who knows which handsome unmarried man might make an appearance this year? We could definitely do with the hope of it.'

Millie blushed and Lottie frowned.

'I know you do not particularly enjoy venturing to see Alexandra, but she has always been kind to me and I like her company. Besides, it is only for a few weeks and the celebration of the Christmas season will lighten things up.'

Privately Lottie thought it would also mean Lady Alexandra would drink more, but for Mama's sake she rallied. Papa had been dead for almost ten years and her mother still talked about him as if he had died only yesterday. A love match. A perfect union. Two halves of a whole. Exactly the thing that Millie would never be allowed to experience should she marry the son of the local vicar, Mr Gilbert Griffiths.

Yet as she stood there a new thought began to form. A startlingly dangerous plan that made her heart race.

Could she risk it? Would it work? The ghost of her father sat there, too, in the room beside her. Henry Fairclough, the fourth son of an earl, would never have allowed his older daughter to make such a compromise. No, Papa would have fought for something shining and wonderful, Lottie knew this completely.

Well, she would, too, but in her own manner. The last time she could remember her sister being excited in the company of a man was eight years ago after a ball in which Amelia had been asked to dance by the mysterious Mr Jasper King. Lottie remembered seeing him through the banisters from the upstairs landing when he had come to pay his regards to her sister the day after. Although Lottie had only been very young at the time, she'd nevertheless understood that she was in the company of a man who had presence. He was tall and dark headed and more than handsome, but it was his certainty and his confidence that she had been struck by the most.

When he had looked up and caught her eyes he'd smiled. To her eternal shame, Lottie had lived off that particular moment for years afterwards. A Prince Charming who had come to rescue them with love and who looked just as she had imagined one would.

But Millie failed to persist with him and Mr King had disappeared from their lives, vague references coming only from Silas, who revered the ground the older engineer stood on. Her brother had worked for the Kings as an apprentice in London for a time before being seconded to their main office in Liverpool, so the ties between Jasper and her family had pretty much been broken, then.

Lottie did know Jasper had a sister who lived on the other side of the city and she had heard a rumour that he would attend a charity Christmas event in London with her in just over a week's time. Even though she knew Amelia was the one who deserved him, she hadn't broken the habit of listening for snippets of information about the man.

The strands of the chance of happiness for her family had begun to unravel and disconnect and just when all seemed to be lost she saw a way of threading them back together again. Could she find Mr Jasper King and lead him in the direction of her sister?

The daring of the escapade worried her a little bit, but Nanny Beth had always said great deeds were usually wrought at great risk. Lottie couldn't remember why Nanny would have had reason to say this, but she had certainly shared it with Lottie many a time before she had passed away at the age of sixty-eight.

Just the thought of such sage advice made her feel better about her whole idea.

'You look like the cat who has the cream, Lottie.' Her mother made this observation and Millie glanced over and frowned.

'What new crazy scheme are you dreaming up now, Lottie? Remember how the last one turned out when you decided to help Mrs Wilson claim her right to be the main character in last year's Christmas pageant at the Foundation?'

'Well, how was I to know she would suffer such

dreadful stage fright and nearly put the whole show in jeopardy?'

'It was lucky Mama knew all the words and that there was a second plan in place that we could revert to.'

A second plan? Well, that was a thought. If by chance she should fail in her intention of dangling the charms of her sister under the nose of Mr Jasper King, she could at least plead she was there to ask if he had any news of her brother.

The day brightened considerably.

'This is your colour, Lottie, for it will bring out the gold in your eyes.' Her mother held the tawny silk before her and Lottie stood still. Unlike Millie, she had never been that interested in fashion and had no true opinion as to what suited her and what didn't. 'I will use the same pattern I found last year with the high neck and wide sleeves. A new dress for each of us will take no time at all and will be so good for one's confidence.'

Lottie looked up at that. She would need confidence to pull this plan off and if this dress gave her an added edge then she was all for it.

'I will help you cut the fabric, Mama. Let me just find my glasses and my pins.'

Chapter Two

Early December 1842

Jasper King lay in bed at his town house on the west side of Arlington Street in Piccadilly overlooking Green Park and watched the smoke rings from his cheroot rise towards the high ceiling and its ornate centre rosette.

He'd moved into this house because he'd felt he needed a base and after years in Liverpool he'd wanted to come home to the city he'd lived in as a child and finally rest for a while. His father would have approved, he thought, smiling as he remembered the man who had brought his children up almost singlehandedly after the death of his wife. Arlene Susan King. His mother. He had not known her so his memories were only from stiff etchings, the sepia images giving little away as to the true nature of the woman. She had always felt like a stranger.

He shook off such melancholy, his thoughts returning to the day at hand. His elder sister Meghan had said she would meet him after two in the afternoon at a Christmas party she had helped organise so he still had a few hours to use up in the meantime. As a man who had been busy for so many years with the engineering firm his father had started, and all its demands, this was an unparalleled indolence, but for once he allowed the sheer silence of living to wash across him as he simply sat and did nothing.

Three years ago at this time he had hit rock bottom, the laudanum calling him home.

Stretching his right leg, he winced. The pain was still there, but the hurt had diluted into the known. He was no longer as whole as he once had been, but the shock had receded somewhat and a sort of resigned acceptance had followed.

Drawing again on his cheroot, he enjoyed the earthy mellow taste of tobacco. He'd have liked a brandy along with it, but had made it his purpose to rise above multiple vices with a dedicated resolve and he seldom gave in to any craving now without a fight. The opium and morphine had long gone and for that he was glad, but he still remembered the hell of a job he'd had to get off it as if it were yesterday.

Three hours until he saw his sister. The contrast between what he was doing and thinking here and now and all the expectations required for later amused him. For so long he'd been a hidden person and the thought of attending a gathering of those with the sole devotion to do good works made him tense. He was far from being a saint.

Lifting up the thin book on his lap, he let it slip to the floor, its spine flattening open on the parquet. *A Journal of a Voyage Round the World.*

Jasper wondered why he read such things, given he had never been to the far-flung destinations Captain James Cook had been wont to in his tiny boat and was hardly likely to, but something inside sought the incredible drama of lives lived to the very edge.

He wanted a release from himself and he reasoned worlds far from his own reality might almost give him that. It was comforting reading about men who risked everything for the pursuit of something far greater than themselves. Men who pushed the boundaries and reaped the results.

The clock on the mantel boomed out the hour of eleven and he watched the minute hand move around the numbers below it. A second. A minute. An hour. A day. A year. A decade. A lifetime.

Lists reassured him because they signified control. One followed the next. In order. In sequence. He could recite all the components of endless directories he'd memorised with ease and often did so.

Was this the beginning of the slide down into despondency? Like his father? That thought worried him and he leaned back against numerous carefully positioned pillows and breathed out.

Even his slumber now held an unchanged and precise structure and he longed to return to the time when he could've slept anywhere. The time when release came simply with the closing of one's eyes.

So many damned years ago. When he was fit and

whole. He grimaced as his foot lost its purchase on the sheets and his injured leg jolted.

A doctor's visit was in order again. He knew it. The metal was still in his thigh, scraping against bone and moving in ways that his body recognised as dangerous. Sometimes he almost wished that which was foreign inside him might just enter into his bloodstream and that would be the end of it. A physician had told him such a catastrophe was eminently possible and the horror he'd once felt at such a warning was waning.

Pushing back the covers, he sat on the side of the bed. He needed to shave and have his hair cut. He needed to lighten up. He needed to live again as though every day might be his last, but Christmas was coming soon and the whole idea of such an enforced joviality made him tired.

Meghan had had a baby earlier in the year and she wanted him to be more of a part of her family life in order to get to know his niece, Sarah. She was worried for him. He could tell that she was.

Just thinking about baby Sarah made him smile. She was fat and hairless and the rings of flesh around all the parts of her body transformed her into a tiny Buddha just waiting for her chance to rule. He'd never thought about children much until meeting her and she had stolen his heart at the very first sight of her toothless smile.

He'd bought a doll's house to give her at Christmas and he'd had small figurines of their family made by a craftsman in Liverpool. His own image had surprised him for in porcelain he looked a lot more gregarious than he felt he ever did in real life. He hoped his sister would like the present for she'd seemed exhausted lately, the chaotic household all about her adding to her fatigue.

He should be more thankful of the silence in his town house, for a few hours in the company of his sister and her offspring usually saw him scrambling back to Piccadilly in relief. The bank drafts he'd arranged each month for Meghan had brought a little escape for her from the constant worry of financial hardship and although Jasper would have liked to have donated more, his sister's husband, Stephen Gibson, was a proud man and had refused the offer. Instead, Jasper had set up a further trust fund for his niece and given Meghan the rights of withdrawal from it.

A knock at his door had him turning and his valet, Hutton, walked in.

'I've clothes for your outing, sir, and would recommend you take the thicker wool coat. It's cold today.'

'Almost snowing.' A quick observation out of the window showed purple clouds on the horizon that were trailing quickly south.

'Your sister sent a note just to reiterate that she will meet you at the address she told you of. She hopes you will not be late.'

'Thank you, Hutton.'

'Very well, sir.' The man hesitated. 'There is another matter, sir. A letter arrived a moment ago and the delivery boy asked if you could see to it straight away.'

Hutton proceeded to place a lilac envelope sealed with wax of the same colour in Jasper's hand. A feminine missive. He recognised the handwriting on the front and his heart sank. Verity Chambers was becoming increasingly forward with her actions in contacting him and he would need to deal with her firmly. However, he could not quite face doing so today.

Balling up the missive, he aimed for the rubbish bin on one side of the room and the small paper flew over in an arc and landed neatly in.

'Well done, sir.'

He smiled. 'That will be all for now.'

He'd made a lucky escape from marriage to Miss Chambers three years ago even though at the time he had not thought it. With renewed purpose Jasper opened his book again and went back to his reading.

Lottie wondered momentarily about the wisdom of walking alone across London to a function she had received no official invitation to attend. Her cough had worsened rapidly and there was a wry irony in that. The weather had worsened as well, the snow that had been holding off now falling lightly. Brushing the gathering flakes from her cloak, she bent her head into the wind.

She had exaggerated her small sickness to escape Lady Malverly's party in the country and pleaded instead to be left at the Fairclough Foundation in the care of her maid until she could join Mama and Amelia in a fortnight's time. Her family had left two days ago and this morning she was suddenly a lot more ill than she wanted to be, but at least the deception had allowed her plan to be put in place.

The small group of youths came from nowhere on the eastern edge of Great Peter's Road and surrounded her, leaving her to clutch her reticule to her chest with more force than she meant.

'Go away, the lot of you.' It never paid to show any sort of fear, but in truth her heart was beating fast. 'Go back to where you belong and leave me alone. I have nothing at all that you could want.'

'Do you not now?' The largest boy at the front looked her over. 'Seems to me you are mighty pretty to be alone.'

'If you touch me, I will hurt you.'

Blackened teeth showed. 'How did you plan to do that? You are a little on the small side.'

'The crushing of a foe holds no correlation with the size of one's muscles. It's all here, you see, in the head. Give me one moment to lay you out flat on the road or be gone. I have no time to tarry.'

Such confidence seemed to quell a little of the bravado displayed by the group and Lottie pushed her advantage.

'Well, hurry up. What's it to be? A fight or the wisdom to retreat?'

'You ain't scared, miss?' A boy from behind the first asked this question, his eyes full of puzzlement.

'Of course not. I see boys just like you around the Fairclough Foundation on Howick Place, but its seldom one has the temerity to threaten me.'

'Miss Fairclough?' Another lanky youth detached himself from the group. 'It's you?'

'Indeed it is.' She squinted to see his face better, not wanting to extricate her spectacles from the bag which had begun all this nonsense in the first place and draw notice to her possessions. 'Who are you?'

'My cousin, Emmeline Fraser, is learning to sew at your school. She loves going there.'

The tone of the group had subtly changed now. It was something to steal from a stranger and quite another thing to do it from a friend.

'Emmeline's mother no doubt would be most upset to hear about this awkward meeting then should I find the need to tell her of it.'

The first challenger had stepped back now and the others had followed. She used such indecision to her advantage.

'Well, I shall bid you all goodbye and I hope next time we see each other it might be in happier circumstances.'

The passageway was opened to her and Lottie stepped through, taking care to lift her skirts over the drain that ran down the middle of the road. The hard anger inside had lessened now, but fright lingered. She really ought to have taken her maid, Claire, with her today as the walk was a reasonable distance and a further fracas was something she did not need.

Smoothing down her golden skirt, she tidied the tendrils of her hair and took in a deep breath.

She could not afford to lose heart if she stood any chance of completing what she had set out to do.

Shoving her thick woollen cloak back, she checked to make sure the note she had spent a long time writing last night was still in her pocket. If words failed her at least, she had this to give him. Mr Jasper King. She hoped all this effort would come to something.

After the unsettling meeting with the street youths Lottie wondered if she could still manage to complete her task. Shaking her head hard, she stepped forward. Of course she could. If she were to fail then her sister Millie would marry a man who was overzealous, ridiculous and pedantic to boot and she would be miserable. Lottie could not let that happen.

After walking another quarter of an hour, the streets held a greater cleanliness and beauty and she loosened her guard a little. Great George Street had a different feel from the narrow dank alleyways that sat in the shadows of Westminster Abbey and she was glad to have arrived there.

Jasper King's sister was called Mrs Gibson, a woman she had met once a few years ago on a committee set up for the Betterment of Women at Risk. Lottie prayed she would remember their association and allow her entrance, but this was just another problem on a day of many. She sniffed and felt red-raw pain sear her throat. She had lost her handkerchief somewhere and had not thought to add a spare to the contents of her reticule.

Her nose was dripping.

Using the back of her hand so as not to stain her dress, she wiped away the moisture, looking up at the house she had finally reached just as the sun came out, its brightness reflecting upon the glass and sending a shaft of light down on the street before her.

Perhaps this was an omen? Perhaps right at this moment Millie was already being courted at the party in the country by a man for whom she could hold a *tendre*. Lottie frowned even as the thought of what she was doing here had her crossing her heart, such a deception probably the worst idea she had ever concocted.

Lady Alexandra's parties had always been full of people for whom Lottie held little liking, with their penchant for the chitter-chatter of nonsense and shared gossip. It had been a relief when Mama had agreed to allow her to stay at home in the company of her maid until she was feeling a bit better.

Jasper King held the answer to all their prayers. He might also know where her brother Silas was, for although she hated to admit to worry, it was most definitely there. Seven months without correspondence was an inordinately long time, even for her adventurous sibling.

Two young women in front of her stopped to look around as she took the first step towards the front door. Dressed beautifully, they gave the impression of questioning her presence here, but Lottie was as easily at home with the rich as she was with the poor.

'Good morning.' Her voice was as friendly as she could make it. 'My goodness, can you believe that it is only a few weeks until Christmas and so very much to do.'

'That is exactly what we were just saying, wasn't it, Rachael? The year just passes by so quickly and suddenly it is the Season of Hard Work again.' The taller woman looked far more agreeable now, holding the door open for Lottie to follow them. Without an invitation in hand she hurried up behind them and continued the conversation, smiling at the stern-looking servant who stood back from the front door and was seeing to cloaks and hats.

'Thank you.' With relief, she accompanied the others into a salon to the right side of the entrance, accepting a glass of white wine from another servant who stood with a silver tray filled with drinks.

The wine fortified her and made her feel warm again, the alcohol bolstering up both courage and anticipation. She knew no one at all, the two women she had spoken to having disappeared off into the far corners of the large salon. Still, she did not falter, looking around with hope as she came inside the room. He had to be here somewhere—Mr King with his velvet eyes and his beautiful smile—but she could not see him, the chatter in the crowd growing with each passing moment as more people arrived. How much did a person change in eight years? She prayed that she would recognise him.

She should put her spectacles on, she knew that, but some sort of personal vanity stopped her from retrieving them from her reticule. 'Best foot forward' resounded in her brain and she smiled as yet another of Nanny Beth's sayings was remembered.

Thank goodness for her new gown, she thought,

and as a wave of missing her mother and sister assailed her she moved on into the back salon proper.

Here the crush was worse than in the front room and, spying a window seat to one side, she made for it and sat. This would be a good vantage point, slightly elevated and comfortable. Her nose had begun to run again and she wiped the end of it with her hand, turning the wet palm into her skirt after she had done so and smiling vapidly.

'Act as if you were born to be a queen,' Nanny Beth used to say when they were children making their annual sojourn to the country and to another Malverly party. If there was anyone with a life that had been more difficult or more broad than her surrogate grandmother's, Lottie had yet to meet them and so any advice was always heeded.

Lifting her chin, she did not waver and when she caught her image in the glass to her left she thought even her normally wayward hair was obeying Nanny's long-ago command. The day spiralled in on her and she closed her eyes for a moment to savour the success of her plan.

'Please Lord, let this work. Please let Mr Jasper King be here among the melee and please let him listen.'

Jasper stood at the top of the landing and looked around. His sister was here somewhere; all the good works she was involved in culminating in this Christmas charity event. Even as he thought this he found

Meghan chatting to this person and laughing with that one.

Civil engineering, the family company, King Enterprises, and the great pressure of work that came with it had made him too busy for all this. He couldn't remember coming anywhere near the social scene much, even before injuring his leg, and he was pleased to see a footman conveying wine.

Good wine, he amended a moment later, and, returning his glass, procured another of the same ilk. Fortified, he could probably do a better job here and he knew his sister would spend a good hour with him afterwards dissecting all the conversations they'd had.

A voice from the past made him turn and there before him stood Miss Susan Seymour, a friend of Verity Chambers, the woman he'd imagined himself to be deeply in love with three years ago before his whole world had fallen to pieces.

'My God, is it you? Mr King? Verity said you were back in London. You do know that she has been trying to get in touch with you, don't you?' Susan Seymour was cut from the same cloth as Verity Chambers, her alabaster skin flawless and her eyes blue. Both had been beautiful women and Susan still was. The light caught the blonde tints in her hair and her high-necked bodice was particularly flattering. 'I cannot quite believe you are back in London in person. You always seemed so immured in the north.'

She moved closer. 'You knew Verity married Mr Johnny Alworthy a month after she left you, but did you also know that he died just over a year ago in an accident?'

The news was unexpected. 'I am sorry. I had not heard that.'

'Oh, it was not the tragedy you might think it,' Susan Seymour returned, her voice low and husky. 'As soon as she was married I think she wished she wasn't. She was always so eminently sensible, but her love affair with Alworthy dissipated all that in a moment and was something I could never understand. Personally, I do not think she can now, either.'

The shocking truth of that statement left him marooned, as did Susan Seymour's hand resting on his arm. The wine quickly drunk was also doing its bit to make him feel dislocated and all he hoped for was that his sister might come looking for him and interrupt.

'It was her mistake to say goodbye to you, of course, and God knows why she did so?' She let that question slide as he failed to answer. 'Verity has not been happy since, so I can only surmise that being young has its pitfalls and they were ones she just could not have possibly predicted.' This was said with intensity as her fingers squeezed his arm. Her eyes were full of question.

Jasper refused to be drawn into explanation. 'Well, now we are all older and much wiser. Thank God.'

'Older, perhaps, but you've created quite a stir here today. I have been hearing your name right across the room.'

'My sister is one of the sponsors—' he said, but Susan Seymour interrupted him, eyes alive in interest.

'I do not think it is your sister the women are interested in. You have built up King Enterprises to be a powerful and well-known company, your influence in all areas of business a common topic of people's conversation. It is *you* they wish to know better, Jasper, a man they admire.'

The use of his Christian name and such overt flirtation had him stepping back. 'When you do see Mrs Alworthy, please tell her that I send my regards, but I am not planning on staying in London for long.'

'Then that is a shame and I know she will be sorry for it. As will I.'

With a forced smile Jasper took his leave and walked towards the large windows on one side of the room. Here at least there was space to breathe, for the conversation with Susan Seymour had shocked him.

'God, help me.' The words escaped unbidden as he stopped and a woman he had failed to see sitting beside him glanced up and stood.

'My thoughts exactly, but you at least look like you fit in here.'

'And you don't?'

She was petite and well formed, her hair a wild bunch of escaping curls and her irises the colour of old whisky. She also had dimples, deep ones in each cheek.

'I am only here to meet someone, but unfortunately I cannot see him anywhere.' As she stated this she craned her neck as though having one final look.

'Who is it? Perhaps I would know of him?'

'Mr Jasper King. He is the owner of an engineering company that builds railways and bridges all across England.' A slight blush covered her cheeks.

The jolt of shock as she mentioned his name came unexpectedly. Jasper was seldom surprised by anyone any more and the feeling took him aback.

'And who are you?'

'Miss Charlotte Fairclough. My sister Amelia and our mama and I run the Fairclough Foundation for needy women and their children in Howick Place in Westminster.'

Through the haze of the past Jasper remembered seeing a younger version of this woman huddled against an upstairs banister as he had come to pay his regards to her sister after some ball. Charlotte? She had had another name then and he sought to recollect it. As if she had read his thoughts she continued.

'But people more often call me Lottie.'

'I think Charlotte suits you better.' God, what the hell had made him say that to her, such a personal and familiar declaration? But if she was startled by his words she certainly did not show it.

'I always thought that, too. For a little while I insisted everyone use my full name but old habits soon crept back in and now hardly anyone uses it. Well, Mama does when she is cross at me, which actually is quite often, but otherwise it is Lottie. Plain and simple.'

The babble of her words was somehow comforting. After the surprise of seeing Susan Seymour and all the undercurrents there, this conversation was easy and different. He leaned back against the wall and decided to stay put for a while. What was it Miss Fairclough wanted of him, though? He could not think of any reason why she would seek him out unless it was something to do with her brother. Before he could be honest and tell her his name she had already gone off on another tangent.

'Are you married, sir?'

'I am not.' He tried to keep the relief from his words.

'But would you want to be? Married, I mean? One day?'

She was observing him as if she were a scientist and he was an undiscovered species. One which might be the answer to an age-old question. One from whom she could obtain useful information about the state of Holy Matrimony.

'It would depend on the woman.' He couldn't remember in his life a more unusual conversation. Was she in the market for a groom or was it for someone else she asked?

'But you are not averse to the idea of it?' She blurted this out. 'If she was the right one?'

Lord, was she proposing to him? Was this some wild joke that would be exposed in the next moment or two? Had the Fairclough family fallen down on their luck and she saw his fortune as some sort of a solution? Thoughts spun quickly, one on top of another and suddenly he'd had enough. 'Where the hell is your brother, Miss Fairclough?'

She looked at him blankly. 'Pardon?'

'Silas. Why is he not here with you and seeing to your needs?'

'You know my brother?'

Her eyes were not quite focused on him, he thought then, and wondered momentarily if she could be using some drug to alter perception. But surely not. The Faircloughs were known near and far for their godly works and charitable ways. It was his own appalling past that was colouring such thoughts.

'I do know him. I employed him once in my engineering firm.'

'Oh, my goodness.' She fumbled then for the bag on the floor in front of her, a decent-sized reticule full of belongings. Finally, she extracted some spectacles. He saw they'd been broken, one arm tied on firmly with a piece of string. When she had them in place her eyes widened in shock.

'It is you.'

'I am afraid so.'

'Hell.'

That sounded neither godly nor saintly and everything he believed of Miss Charlotte Fairclough was again turned upside down.

Chapter Three

Jasper King had fallen into her lap, so to speak, and if he had been handsome all those years ago as she'd observed him from her eyrie on the stairs, then now he was breathtaking. No longer a boy but a man, his edges rougher, his eyes darker, the danger that had once been only a slight hint around him now fully formed, hewn into menace. Seasoned. Weathered.

He was beautiful.

Looking around, Lottie could see that almost all the other women in the room had made the same kind of assessment, for eyes everywhere were upon him.

The fluster of her mistake and the splendour of her companion made her blush, a slow rolling redness that would be inescapable against the fairness of her skin. She wished she could have been more urbane, less ruffled. She wished the ground beneath her might have opened and simply swallowed her up, but of course it didn't and she was forced to cope.

The cough she had been afflicted with suddenly

decided at that moment to become unbridled, and one small cough turned into a minute-long hack, sweat beading her body with its growing intensity.

He passed her his own drink, a white wine that was as dry as it was strong. She swallowed the lot, praying to God that her infirmity might cease as tears of exertion ran from the corners of her eyes. Dabbing at them with her fingers, she faced him.

'I have been ill, but…our family is swiftly running…out of both money and hope…as Silas seems to have vanished…off the very face of the earth.' These bare bones of stated truth were given succinctly as she laid out her family's present predicament without embroidering it. She was finding breathing difficult and was struggling to keep another coughing fit at bay. She felt too hot as well…from the blush or from a rising fever? At that particular moment she could not tell which was the culprit. She did not feel up to throwing her sister's name into the mix, for her confused hope and dread of Jasper falling madly in love with Amelia all over again were at this moment too complex and disjointed to explain properly.

He frowned and pushed dark hair back from his face. His hands were as beautiful as the rest of him. He wore a solid ring of gold on the fourth finger of his right hand with an engraving of sorts etched into it.

'I had a letter from your brother two months ago. Silas sounded hale and hearty.'

'Only two months?' The relief of his words made her feel faint all over again. 'Then he is not dead. Millie could no longer feel his presence in the world, you see, and as a twin that was a decided worry and even Mama, who is normally so very sensible, had begun to have a haunted look in her eyes and…' She stopped, taking in breath. 'I cannot believe it. You are sure it was only two months ago?'

'I am.'

'Then why would he have not written to us to let us know where he was, how he was? He must have known our fears?'

'He sounded busy. He sounded as if he was in the process of finalising a business scheme in Baltimore that he was sure was going to make him a fortune.'

Could it possibly be this easy? Suddenly all Lottie wanted to do was to be the bearer of such good news and send a message promptly to Mama and Millie. They would be as thrilled as she had been and as puzzled probably, too, but Silas's whole disappearance began to make a certain sense. He'd always struggled with commitment and tying himself down. She imagined him in some far-flung uncivilised colony of the Americas, a long way from anywhere that dealt with post or a port by which mail might have been conveyed.

'Are you well, Miss Fairclough?' His words registered amid all her rushing conjectures and she turned back to him.

'I am indeed, Mr King. Better, in fact, than I have been for a very long while even with the affliction of this cough that has become worse so very quickly. My brother's disappearance has been weighing on me as if it were a large stone tied on my back, you see, and it's like that old adage, I expect—the one that says "Worry often gives a small thing a great shadow".'

This time he laughed out loud and a number of people turned to look at them.

'I have never heard that before. Where is it from?'

'It is an ancient Swedish proverb, I think. My Nanny Beth used it.'

'She is still alive? God, I remember her.'

'No. She died six years ago. On earth one day and in heaven the next. Silas said it was such a fitting death for one who in life had never wanted a fuss.'

Again he laughed and the darkness in his eyes lifted. That was what was different, Lottie thought, his eyes. Last time she had seen them they had been full only of lightness.

A woman she recognised as Jasper King's sister was then suddenly at his side and looking at her quizzically.

'Do I know you? Your face is familiar.'

Lottie held out a hand. 'I am from the Fairclough Foundation in Howick Place and I knew your brother briefly, once.'

'Very briefly,' Jasper added, 'but our reacquaintance has been most enlightening.'

He did not sound as though he quite believed this and Lottie turned to his sister, trying to cover the awkwardness. Another woman had also joined their small group, a beautiful blonde woman with cornflower-blue eyes and a sweet smile. She looked at Jasper as if she wanted to eat him up and, sensing she was now a little in the way, Lottie smiled.

'Well, if you will excuse me I shall go and find a drink. I have a cough.'

'Yes, we all heard.' The other woman's words were not kind. 'I very much hope that you do not spread it around just before Christmas.'

'And I hold the very same hope.'

Without looking back at the others Lottie threaded her way through the room, making for the door. The news of her brother did not allow even the rudeness of the beautiful woman to penetrate her euphoria and all she wanted to do was to make for home and send word to Mama and Millie about this wonderful new discovery of Silas's wellbeing.

Alive. Well. Prospering even. Their trials and tribulations would soon be at an end and Amelia would not have to marry the curate after all.

Collecting her hat and heavy cloak, she fastened both upon her person and tilted her head against the growing wind outside. At least it had stopped snowing and a return journey always seemed much quicker.

Digging her hands into her pocket, she felt the long letter that she had written. She had not thought to give it to Jasper King, but at least such an omission gave Amelia the chance to meet him properly at some point and who knew what might come from that.

A cloud made the day darken and she bit at her bottom lip. Amelia was far more beautiful than she was and after this meeting all Jasper King must have comprehended about her was oddness. He was probably laughing with his sister and the beauty right at this moment as he retold the story to the others of her gauche outbursts and of her peculiar manner.

Not her finest hour, Lottie thought with a sadness, and wished with every piece of her heart that she could have started this afternoon all over again.

She was nowhere in the room. She had gone. After looking round the front parlour and failing to find her, Jasper strode to the entrance where an elderly servant was waiting to dispense coats and hats.

'Did Miss Fairclough leave?'

'The young lady with the curls?' The man waited as Jasper nodded. 'She did indeed, sir, a good ten minutes ago now. But it seems to me that she hailed no carriage, setting out to walk instead.' His eyes strayed to the window. 'In this weather the young lady's journey will be a cold one.'

Anger tightened his chest. Miss Charlotte Fairclough would walk all the way from here to Howick Place on one edge of the Irish Rookery in this weather? It was a decent distance and the journey would take her through many of the less salubrious parts of the city. Asking for his coat and hat, he put them on and walked outside, gesturing to the driver of his waiting carriage. The icy crunch of freezing snow beneath his boots worried him.

Five minutes later he found her walking down St Anne's Street. She was coughing again, he could see that by the way she was hunched in with her body shaking. Did the younger Fairclough have no sense whatsoever? Leaning out of the window, he instructed his man to pull in just ahead of her, glad to see that she came to a standstill when he got out and was waiting patiently as he approached her.

'Do you wish to be struck down with pneumonia, Miss Fairclough?' He looked pointedly up at the sky. The snow had turned into sleeted rain now, driving in from the north with force.

Her head shook, the curls dripping like sodden rat tails where they fell beneath the hat she now wore.

'I d-do n-not.'

She was shaking so hard she could barely get her words out, and the fury that he had felt when first seeing her trudging homewards doubled.

'Get into my carriage. I shall take you home.'

She did as he ordered, sitting down primly and folding her cloak tighter in around her, though as he followed her in his damn leg gave way and he almost toppled into her lap, saving himself from doing so at the very last moment.

The talkative Miss Fairclough seemed to have disappeared altogether. This version was a far quieter one, watching him with those whisky eyes of hers in a careful and cautious manner.

'The forecast is for heavier snow and the temperatures are plummeting. I doubt your brother would be pleased to see you traipsing in this part of London town alone and in such weather.'

The mention of Silas brought her glance to his. 'You are right, Mr King. It was foolish.'

'Surely someone should have accompanied you today. A maid? Your mother?'

'My mother, Lilian, is in the country at a Christmas party of Lady Alexandra Malverly's and my sister has journeyed with her.'

'But you were not invited?'

The same slight blush he had noticed when talking with her before resurfaced.

'I was sick.'

'Which is even more of a reason to be warm indoors.'

The heat in the conveyance seemed to have aggravated her illness and he waited again for a moment until she stopped coughing, her hands winding into the material of her skirt and bunching it into tight folds. She looked like a small wet angel blown in by the winter chills, her hair all loose and her cheeks weather reddened. As he took in the curves of her body beneath the folds of her cloak, he glanced away. His right leg ached and his meeting with Susan Seymour sat firmly in his mind.

Miss Verity Chambers had broken off their engagement summarily after knowing the extent of an injury she could not abide. A note had arrived from her, the physician delivering it to his bedside along with the morphine. The shock had almost killed him.

God. He shifted his leg towards the carriage door, the altered angle helping ease the pain. He could walk again at least and the broken nerves did not jump into trauma with as much regularity as they had before.

But he was still a damaged man, inside and out— a man who could destroy Miss Charlotte Fairclough with all her joy and natural exuberance just by being who he was.

Leaning forward, he threaded his fingers together. He would drop her off at the Foundation and leave. He would also write to her brother and let him know the family circumstances for he could not believe that the honourable young man he had once known well would leave them all so very much in need. He also wondered if they would accept an interim loan in the meantime from him, but did not know quite how to phrase such an offer without it sounding like charity.

Glancing out of the window, Jasper took in a breath and tried not to be mesmerised by the scent of lavender and lemon that was not quite submerged under the heavier odour of soaking wet wool.

He was scowling again, the laughing man she had warmed to at the charity event completely swallowed up by this ill-tempered one admonishing her at every turn.

It was still a few minutes at least until they reached Howick Place and Lottie wished she might have refused this ride altogether.

The trouble was, there was something about him that she felt a connection to, a connection that she had understood eight years before sitting at the top of the stairs and spying upon him as he had come calling upon her sister.

He limped badly. She had noticed this as he had led her into the carriage a few moments before and once she was inside she saw his hand drop to his right thigh and rest there. For support? For balance? Lottie had thought he was going to fall for a second when he had first joined her in the conveyance, but he'd recovered his equilibrium just in time to sit, heavily, eyes flaring in pain and anger as he'd looked away.

His rigid control was worrying for he was a man so unlike the memory of her gentle and loving father that for a moment she felt bewildered by her notice of him.

'I am sorry to have been a nuisance to you, Mr King.'

She wanted to also add that he could let her out now but, in the light of the worsening weather, did not quite feel up to plodding the rest of her way home.

The tears filling her eyes surprised her. She seldom cried. Perhaps it was a mixture of relief over the knowledge of her brother's recent letter and of the day's convoluted happenings. Taking in a deep breath, she tried to temper her reaction and ended up with another fit of coughing.

Goodness, was she really much sicker than she thought and could she be spreading it to him even as she sat there?

When he handed over a clean white handkerchief she was surprised.

'Nothing is ever as bad as you might think it, Miss Fairclough.'

It was monogrammed with his initials and pressed into such starched precise folds she hardly dared unravel it.

'Thank you.'

He nodded, waiting until she had blown her nose before speaking again.

'This weather will improve tomorrow.'

She had the distinct feeling that he was filling in the awkward gaps and giving her time to recover. He certainly had not mentioned her tears and for that Lottie was relieved. She sought to find some conversational small talk of her own.

'The blonde woman with her hand on your arm at the charity event looked very beautiful.'

He did not answer.

'Your sister looks kind, too.'

'She is.'

'I seldom go to these large affairs in town because they are always rather daunting. Mama is the one who more usually attends them, but she cancelled her invitation because she was going to the Malverlys' instead. She enjoys Lady Malverly's happy disposition, I suppose, because it is a welcome change from all the never-ending problems at the Foundation.'

At that he frowned.

'Is Mr Septimus Clarke still there as the General Manager? I remember him as a man who had been there for a very long time.'

'No, he retired last year and Mr Jerome Edwards has taken over his position.'

'A new employee, then?'

'But one who comes well recommended. He will be pleased to hear of Silas's return, no doubt, so if there was any chance of seeing my brother's letter,

Mr King, I would like to show it to him. It might set his mind to rest regarding the funds.'

'Of course. I shall have the correspondence delivered to you, Miss Fairclough.'

So formal. The chill of distance was back. She wished Jasper might laugh again or at least smile, but mostly she wished he might touch her as he had when he'd helped her into the carriage.

There it was again, that ridiculous sense of notice of him which had no place at all in her life. He was rich, beautiful and well connected and he had numerous women clambering after him. He was also a man who, at this moment, looked at if he was desperate to escape the cloying closeness of the conveyance and her company in particular.

People found her odd. Lottie knew that they did. She was too rebellious and independent and did not have the charitable patience of Millie or the over-reaching goodness of her mother. She'd do anything to protect the women they helped, but sometimes, like Silas, she wanted more.

More of a life and an opportunity to see other places and meet other people. More of a chance to read and discover and know things that she knew she now did not.

The Foundation was finally in sight, at least, but as she waited for the carriage to slow in front of it she saw Jasper King focus on something that was happening to one side.

When she looked over she was horrified to see Mrs Rosa O'Brian hurrying towards them, very underdressed for a freezing London day. She stopped as Lottie banged her knuckles against the window and opened the carriage door.

'Oh, thank the Lord you are still here, Miss Lottie. I had a feeling you may have gone to the country with Miss Millie and your mother for the Christmas party. I remembered you speaking of it.'

When they alighted Lottie realised Jasper was there, too, right beside her, his large frame sheltering her from the freezing wind. Rosa was now weeping, highly distressed by something. Lottie could never remember her being quite so hysterical.

'It's Harriet White. She is missing and I think I might know exactly where she is.' Her Irish brogue was strong, but Lottie had spent a good amount of time in her company to easily understand what she was saying.

'Missing?' It took her a few seconds to place this word into some sort of order and her heart lurched.

Rosa nodded and as she burst into louder sobs Jasper King looked away. Perhaps he had had enough of crying women today, Lottie thought. Perhaps he was at the very end of his tether with feminine histrionics. She half-expected him to simply return to his carriage, call the driver on and disappear. But he did not. Instead he stood there in the wind without even reaching for his hat.

'Where do you think she is?' Lottie asked this of Rosa gently, trying to understand exactly what 'missing' meant.

'Old Pye Street is where she is and you know what happens there?'

A further distressed howl followed these words and, looking at Jasper, Lottie saw his puzzlement. With little option but to explain she did.

'It is an area quite close that is renowned for its prostitution. It is not a good place for a young woman to be at all, for there are people there who would take advantage of innocence.'

Probably the females of his acquaintance didn't know of such debauchery, let alone mention it. But Lottie had been brought up alongside the women and children the Foundation helped and things such as these were a known entity in everybody's life. Good and evil co-existed simultaneously and it was only a short step from respectability and righteousness into disaster and ruin should circumstances conspire against one.

A man like Mr Jasper King might have little grasp of the precariousness of living at the bottom with his grander upbringing and his wider social circles. Rosa's face, for example, was marked with scars from a relationship that had soured in her early twenties. She looked nothing like the woman Lottie had noticed holding on to Jasper's arm at the charity event they had just been to. In truth, when Lottie had first set eyes upon Rosa's visage even she had been shocked.

And yet Mr King did not move away. Rather he questioned Rosa more closely.

'What brings you to think this woman—Harriet

White was it?...' he waited till Rosa nodded '...that she might be in this particular place?'

'Mr Wilkes, who works at the laundry, said as much, sir. He said there had been whispers of it and that he would not be surprised because Harriet is the sort of girl who might be persuaded to...' She stopped and blushed.

'I see.' When Jasper said this his words were tight and Lottie hurried in herself.

'Then we must go there right now, Rosa. We must go and ask Frank Wilkes exactly what it was he heard and try to find out where she is. Harriet is a special friend of mine, you see,' she added, turning to Jasper King. 'She came to the Foundation as a young girl and we grew up together, and although she sometimes can be a little wild we shared a lot of the same dreams. If anything has happened to her...' She could not finish the obvious and swallowed. 'I have to help her.'

Grabbing her reticule from the carriage floor, she positioned her hat more firmly on her head, but Mr King stopped her as she took the first step away.

'Where do you think you are going? To the laundry? To do what?' He did not sound happy as he loomed above her.

'To try to find out what has happened, of course.'

'Alone? You are going to go there alone? Have you no sense? What happens when the pimp hears of your questions and the brothel owner is affronted? What then? These men are not honourable adversaries—they are hardened criminals and you would be no match at all for them.'

'So I am supposed to just leave it at that. Allow Harriet to be used and then discarded? Allow her to simply throw her young life away?'

'How old is she?'

'Nineteen.'

'And how old are you?'

'Twenty-two.'

'Only three years' difference and you think I should allow you to throw your life away in a sense-less and stupid attempt to make it otherwise. This is not the sort of thing you should be getting yourself mixed up with, Miss Fairclough, and if your brother was here he would say the very same thing. Under no circumstances whatsoever should you go to that laundry and especially not by yourself.'

The controlling way Jasper said these words made Lottie stand on her tiptoes and face him directly.

'You cannot stop me—besides, I have no care for your opinion. Harriet White is my friend and she needs help so I am going whether you like it or not.'

Rosa beside them was crying constantly now, her nose running and her eyes red, and the rain suddenly decided to step up a notch and turn into a downpour.

'Then get in. Both of you. How far is it to this laundry?'

Lord, Jasper thought, save me from women who have no sense or wisdom. The fact that Charlotte Fair-clough would even consider the prospect of going into battle alone infuriated him, but he could not allow the consequences that might follow without making an effort to restrain her.

He would go into Old Pye Street himself to try to find the missing Harriet White and God help anyone who tried to fob him off once he was at his destination.

The scars on the face of the woman opposite pulled at his heartstrings, too, he supposed. Those on his legs were bad enough, but at least they were not on display for the whole entire world to see. Charlotte Fairclough now had her hand entwined through Rosa's and was patting the top of it in an effort to calm her down, though it did not seem to be doing much good.

Did she not see how small she was, how impossibly delicate? How was it she did not recognise the danger of striking out to right all the injustices in the underbelly of London town? Her curls had fallen out further so that it barely looked as if any hair was left pinned up. She was coughing again, too, and that worried him. Miss Fairclough should be at home tucked up in bed with a hot lemon toddy and some tender loving care. Yet here she was in wet boots that looked as if they had seen better days and a cloak with patches upon the pockets. The rain had made her cold because she was shaking and he noticed she swallowed often in between her coughing fits as if to beat back tears. Or take in air.

She was nothing like anybody else he had ever met. Even Verity Chambers, whom he had once thought perfect, sensible and polite, would not have struck out to help another in the way Charlotte Fairclough had. He grimaced.

How did she do this to him so easily, raise an ire that had been largely indifferent or dormant for years? He swore under his breath and thought with resignation that it was turning into a full-time occupation just trying to keep Silas Fairclough's stubborn sister safe.

Chapter Four

Frank Wilkes was taciturn and silent on first meeting, but under the pressure of their questions he did open up a little.

'It were Jack Nisbett who said he'd seen her, Miss Fairclough. He said he had noticed Miss White in Old Pye Street. He said that perhaps she were in one of the upstairs rooms there. When I told Mrs O'Brian what I had discovered she cried and ran out of the place with a stack of laundry to finish by tonight to boot. I am that glad to see her back, mind.'

'I am sorry, Mr Wilkes.' Rosa stepped forward and began collecting a large pile of unfolded clothes heaped across a long table. 'I'll see to these straight away.'

Charlotte Fairclough, meanwhile, stepped from foot to foot and gave the impression that all she wanted to do now was to run and begin her search. Jasper moved across to stand beside her and took her arm, anchoring her in place. Unexpectedly she allowed him to, waiting as he got a blow-by-blow account of the environs from Wilkes.

Local knowledge was always invaluable, the many years of working in his civil engineering firm attesting to that fact. When he had a good idea of the layout of Old Pye Street he turned to Charlotte.

'What exactly does this Harriet White look like?'

'She is tall and thin and she has bright gold hair. Her eyes are brown and she has a birthmark just here.' Charlotte touched her own chin to one side. 'It is a mark in the shape of a small circle.'

Such a particular description heartened Jasper. Surely someone would have recognised the girl and could give him information.

'Right then, you stay here and leave me to it. I will be back within the hour.' He turned to Frank Wilkes. 'Is it possible to give Miss Fairclough a cup of tea? She has been coughing badly and it might soothe her throat.'

'No. I am going with you. I won't be left here. I need to be helping.' Her voice was strong and certain.

'You will help me by staying out of the way and by being safe.'

But Charlotte shook her head fiercely. 'If you leave me here, I will simply follow you, Mr King. Two sets of eyes are far better than one and I can identify Harriet no matter what. If she has dyed her hair…'

'I can look for the birthmark.'

'Which could be easily covered in make-up. There is no telling what she might look like now, but I would know Harriet anywhere. You, on the other hand, have never met her.'

Such a rationale was persuasive. 'Should I agree

to this you have to give me a promise that you will stay out of the way and if there is any trouble you will run back to my carriage as quick as your legs can carry you.'

'Agreed.'

'Hell.'

He was going to let her come and if anything happened because of it he would never forgive himself. Neither would her brother.

Jasper King's size was comforting and the limp he was afflicted with gave him an added danger. He was a man who had known battle and pain, yet lived. He gave no impression at all of a nob who was out of his depth as he strode through the crooked pathways crossing the intersecting labyrinths that led into Old Pye Street.

The place was dank and wet and any daylight was swallowed up by the narrow thinness of the buildings above them, a Stygian stinking gloom all that was left.

An older woman with a basket attached by straps to her back was the first person he talked to.

'We are looking for a young friend of ours, a girl with blonde hair and a birthmark on her chin. She would be new around here and frightened, perhaps.'

'Whores all look the same, sir. Frightened at first, but resigned before long. The money's what brings 'em and it ain't called the Old Pye Street for nothing.'

'So you haven't seen her?'

As she shook her head Charlotte began to speak.

'She is a good girl even if she has been foolish and any help would be very welcome.'

'The One Tun public house is five doors down. Perhaps you might look in there for the patrons of many of the places hereabouts are often found drinking in that establishment. You might be able to ask them.'

'Thank you.' Jasper's voice was deep and he passed a penny over to the woman whose demeanour changed remarkably as a result.

'Ask for Mr Twigg. Tell him Annie sent you. If anyone has seen her, he will have.'

Then she was gone, trudging down the alley with her large basket and calling out to those about her to sample the wares.

'It's a start,' Charlotte said to Jasper as he took her arm and led her on. 'I'd forgotten just how easily a coin loosens the tongue.'

'And I have many more of them, Miss Fairclough.'

She liked his smile and she liked the way his fingers tightened around her wrist. In protection. She'd never have been able to manage this alone despite her telling him the opposite. It wasn't that every person they passed looked as if they might do them harm, but more the understanding that a woman alone would have been fair game for those with a mind for the sort of activity the road was renowned for. She was thankful beyond words to have him striding along beside her.

The One Tun pub was wreathed in the mist of tobacco smoke, with a one-legged man just inside the door begging for alms. Jasper laid another penny in the tattered hat and she saw him tip his head in a shared understanding. Then another was in front of them, a heavy man with a reddened face and a receding hairline.

'I'm after Mr Twigg. Annie sent me.'

Interest passed across his eyes and he led them to a table, signalling for them to sit.

'That'd be me, then, so what's your business?'

'We are looking for a girl who is new to Old Pye Street. Harriet White. She was taken from the laundry in Horseferry Road and we want her back.' He gave Harriet's description and the man pondered it.

'A birthmark, you say, and right here?'

'You've seen her, then?'

'Just for a moment, but from memory her name were not Harriet and the last I saw of her were when she went off in a carriage with a fine toff who had a crest painted on the side of it and all.'

'A crest?' The surprise in Jasper's voice was plain to hear.

'That happens to the new ones sometimes. The ones who are not spoiled or pockmarked or difficult are picked out by gentlemen who can pay a bit more for hanky-panky elsewhere. Sometimes the girls return, but more often they do not.'

The danger of it all was horrifying to Lottie. To simply disappear in a conveyance for relations with a man who was neither known nor honourable seemed to her the very height of foolishness. And Harriet had never seemed to be that.

'Can you tell us of the crest, its design or anything

on it that caught your eye?' Jasper had asked this
question and Lottie waited for the answer.

'There was a helmet and stripes of red and gold,
I think. I only saw it briefly, mind, and so it might
have been something else.'

'Thank you.' Jasper passed over more coins to
Twigg and stood, helping Charlotte up as he did so.
'If there is any news of the girl, could you send me
word here? You would be well remunerated.'

A card was placed on the table.

'Of course, Mr King. I shall make certain that you
know of it.'

Outside Lottie lifted her skirts slightly to step
across the drain, pleased that they were leaving the
place as she breathed in deeply, the smoke of the tavern a thickness in her throat.

A minute later they were inside the King carriage
and as the door closed behind them Lottie let out a
sigh of part-relief.

'Thank you for accompanying me. I could never
have managed that alone.'

'I am glad I could be of help, Miss Fairclough,
and if I hear anything at all from Twigg I will be
in touch.'

'You do not think the man in the carriage will
hurt her?'

She did not like his lack of answer.

'It is a disaster,' she continued as her imagination
raced. 'These awful things happen all about us and
we can only watch them unfold until there is nothing left to do. People simply disappear and never

come back. Young girls. Good girls. Girls who have no one there to watch over them and make certain they are safe.'

Dread consumed her. Harriet was not the first girl to be lost into the world of prostitution and would not be the last either. Lottie felt hopelessly unprepared and impossibly adrift in her anxiety.

She pulled Jasper's handkerchief from her pocket and wiped her nose, pleased that at least for the past half an hour she had not suffered another coughing fit. She wondered if she should give it back to him or if she should take it home to be laundered. She decided on the second option and tucked it again into her cloak.

She could not think of one other person who would have helped her as this man just had. Oh, granted, he had castigated her for the actions she had planned to take, but he had also supported her need to find Harriet when he realised that he could not stop her and ventured without further complaint into places that were foreign and difficult. It had been his coin that had greased the wheels for information without a doubt.

'I shall pay you back,' she suddenly uttered.

'For what?' His eyes were upon her, sliced in puzzlement.

'The payments for information. I cannot expect you to take the burden of that.'

He laughed. 'I assure you, Miss Fairclough, that I can afford it.'

At that she blushed because, conversely, he knew

that she could not. The day was running down now into the evening, the night-time darkness coming in early at this time of the year, and she felt a desolation that was all-consuming.

Would she ever see Jasper King again or would he disappear to the far-off places that were the domain of a successful civil engineer and be lost to her altogether?

The visage of the beautiful blonde woman came to mind. She knew he was not married, but did he have someone who he was fond of waiting for him at home, some mistress of the same ilk as the ones who had gazed at him with longing at the afternoon's charity event?

He would hardly be running to Charlotte's side again after all this. Still, she could not give up the hope of it entirely.

'I shall be at the Foundation for another week before I leave to join my mother and sister. If anything were to come up that concerned Harriet White's whereabouts, I would be most eager to know of it.'

'You shall be the first person I inform, Miss Fairclough.'

'Thank you, Mr King.'

The formality was back, as was the distance.

Already her street was in view and the brick walls of the Foundation could be seen. Another minute and he would be gone.

Impulsively she took his hand in hers, surprised by the warmth of it.

'I should like to say that I am most grateful and

that without your help, Mr King, I doubt I would have achieved anything at all.'

'It is music to my ears to be hearing such a turn-around,' he replied, his mouth twitching.

'My family would probably say that, too,' she returned, and knew it to be true.

Mama would like Jasper King. He was strong and determined and his own man. There were secrets there, she supposed, his leg for one and why he had not married.

She had heard once he was engaged to be wed and wondered what had happened to that relationship. She remembered Silas saying Jasper's father had been sick for a very long time as well and that father and son were close.

All snippets of Jasper's life were fascinating and she wished she knew more. None the less, she had survived today finding out that her brother was still alive and that Harriet White had been carried out of Old Pye Street in a crested carriage which was a clue that could be followed up to find her. She hadn't had a coughing fit for at least an hour and the tightness in her chest that had begun this morning was starting to loosen.

All in all, it had been an unsettling day and almost every emotion she had experienced had something to do with the enigmatic Mr Jasper King. She felt uncertain as to what she felt about him and resolved to leave the letter she had written of her sister's need for a husband in her pocket and see how the rest of it played out. Jasper King did not seem like a man who might be persuaded to do anything he did not want to and the thought of him falling at the feet of her beautiful sister and offering marriage was not at this moment as appealing as it once had been.

When the carriage pulled up in front of the Foundation and he opened the door she saw that he was saying goodbye without coming in. Then he called the driver on.

In another moment he was gone altogether.

His sister Meghan arrived at his town house an hour later and her face was full of questions.

'Who on earth was she, Jasper? I have met her before, I know it, and she said she's from the Fairclough Foundation, but I cannot quite place her face.'

He knew who she spoke of but played along, not particularly wanting the advice he knew she would be doling out next.

'Miss Susan Seymour. She was a friend of Verity Chambers.'

'Not her.'

His sister swiped at his arm and finished her drink, dropping herself on the sofa opposite his chair and holding her glass out for another.

'The one with the wild curls and the golden eyes. The interesting one.'

'Miss Charlotte Fairclough.'

'Oh, my, of course. I met her a year or more ago at some event and she charmed everyone there. Isn't she just so very beautiful?'

Jasper got up to cross to the drinks cabinet, wincing as his leg caught.

'It's sore? Your leg? I have told you again and again to go back to the doctor. I am sure after all this time medical science has moved along and, who knows, there could be a cure for your problems.'

At least talk of his leg had diverted his sister from extolling the charms of Charlotte Fairclough though he knew also that state of affairs would not last for long.

'I'm fine, Meghan.'

'No, Jasper, you are not, but you were always stubborn and have become even more so with age. How on earth did you meet Miss Fairclough?'

'I know her brother Silas—you may remember we took him on as an apprentice some years ago— but today was the first time I have spoken with her.'

'That ghastly Susan Seymour was so rude, wasn't she? As rude as Verity Chambers could be at times, in my opinion, and God knows you should have been thrilled to be untangled from her wiles. I know I was certainly pleased to hear of it despite your feelings for her.'

Jasper smiled at his sister's loyalty. At the time he had been heartbroken and very sick. A collapse of spirit and body had been a hard thing to recover from. Now he agreed with his sister. A marriage between Verity and himself would never have worked but that thought, too, had been a long time in coming.

'I worry about you, Jasper. I worry that you are

too alone, too isolated and too hardened to see that truth. If Papa was here—'

He didn't let her finish. 'Well, he isn't.'

'He wanted to die in the end. Did you know that?' This was new.

'After your accident, when you could not care for him and I came up, he said that four years was long enough for you to be his nursemaid. He wanted you to travel to all those places you'd dreamed about and instead…' She stopped. 'Instead you were glued to his side providing all the care that I could not because he would not leave Liverpool and come to London.'

'It wasn't quite that simple, Meg, and you know it.'

'Then how was it, Jasper? It seemed to me that he was selfish and you were the one who took the whole brunt of it.'

'He was sick and forgetting things and you had lost baby after baby and were just about as ill. He wouldn't have coped somewhere new and you could not have managed with all his needs. Then when I was no longer there—'

His sister did not let him finish. 'He'd had enough when I came up to stay that last time. He said that he was proud of us. But I've told you all that?'

'Probably.'

Jasper couldn't remember this, but then he couldn't remember much about that terrible time. Meghan had arrived in Liverpool just as their father was dying and a matter of months after his own accident. The beginning of the years of hell. The dreams that he'd had across that time still came sometimes and he woke sweating.

'Will you see her again?'

The constant change in topic was a hallmark of his sister's conversation.

'Miss Fairclough? I doubt it. She is very busy at her Foundation, saving lost souls.'

'Then she should be an expert in saving yours,' Meghan shot back, 'and God knows you could do with an angel.'

They had always been close, Meghan and himself, her five years on him having the effect of making her almost like a mother. She gave him advice on everything.

'You need someone you can love, Jasper, someone kind and true and sensible. Someone who can give you children and make up for all those lonely years...'

He stopped her. There were some things that were private between them and this was one of those. Such a thought cut close to the bone and he finished his own drink in one swallow. He wouldn't have another.

'I am off back to Liverpool after the Christmas season and won't be back in London for at least a few months. There is a job in Manchester that is complex.'

Meghan frowned noticeably. 'I see.'

'I know that tone. What do you see?'

'That you do not wish to talk of Miss Charlotte Fairclough with me, which in itself is surprising because it leads me to surmise two things...' She stopped with a pregnant pause.

'And what are they?'

'That the woman is more important to you than you make out she is and that you are running away from anything that might add up to commitment.'

'Meghan?'

'Yes, Jasper?'

'Have another brandy and tell me about Sarah.'

Of all the topics in the world this was the one that always succeeded in shifting Meghan from one thought across to the next.

'She is almost taking a step—did I tell you that? She was leaning on the big floral chair in my sitting room and I turned away and the next moment I saw her let go and hover there, trying to understand the motion...'

Half an hour later his sister was gone, hurrying back to her house to see the child who was the love of her life. Jasper frowned at the way she almost never mentioned her husband in his company and wondered if things were as rosy with Stephen as she had once painted them. Meghan had her secrets, too, but at least she had a daughter whose very existence lit up her world and for that he was glad.

The rain still fell outside and the fire in the grate was burning bright. He watched the sparks at the back of the chimney flare and die and then reappear elsewhere. He wondered if Charlotte Fairclough was warm enough in the big and draughty Fairclough Foundation building on Howick Place. He remembered it as austere and spartan, any luxury stripped from the place in the overriding need to provide for so many desperate people. The family had had a small abode at the back of the place in the days when he knew Silas, but it had been as humble and sparse as the main building.

God, the woman had got under his skin and that was unusual. He'd never met someone so infuriating and so vulnerable all at the same time.

Verity Chambers had sent yet another note and this one had caught him at a time when he had deigned to open it, their shared hopes from the past spilling out on paper and her own apology at such appalling behaviour.

Once he might have drunk the words like a man does water lost in a desert, but now all he could feel was the hurt, pain and guilt. She had crucified him with her easy deceit and he would never allow anyone to do so again.

The clock in the corner boomed out the hour of seven and far off he could see flashes of lightning, the undulating outline of the distant hills of Surrey showing up. He counted the seconds until the thunder came. One, two, three, four, five, six, seven, eight. A long way off, then.

He wished for a moment he might have had a dog to sit by the hearth with him, a warm and breathing body that he could love. But his life was too nomadic, too uncertain and he could not abandon an animal like that into the care of his servants for months at a time as he travelled the country. Still, the idea stuck as he imagined a loyal haughty Newfoundland or a finely bred English bloodhound sitting there watching him. It would be well behaved…unlike Miss Fairclough.

Today had been an adventure and the sort of day he would remember for a long time. As he dozed he pictured fine brown curls and golden-brown eyes and he smiled. It had been a while since he had felt this happy.

Hours later Jasper was sweating when he jolted himself awake, his heart beating at twice its normal speed and the cramps in his right leg making him nauseous. He had not had such intense and inescapable dreams for a while now, the blackness all around and the depraved imaginings fuelled by his experiences with laudanum, opium and morphine. He'd spent two years after his accident in the opium dens trying any sort of narcotic that became available to banish the pain in his thigh: lost years, debauched years, years of misery and ruin. He was not proud of such a fall. Sex, violence and excess were the codes of his life until he had fallen into a coma and Meghan had brought him home.

He owed his sister his life. His new life. The life of strict principles and few vices. He hadn't even been fully present for the last month of his father's existence much to his eternal regret, the cocktail of drugs taking him away.

He needed water, but couldn't make himself get up and he did not want to ring for a servant. So he sat there breathing deeply and trying to find a steadiness and a normality.

He couldn't understand why the dreams were back with such a force.

Fear, perhaps, or the knowledge of some fundamental change within him. His sister's words were there, too, tangled in honesty, snarling with truth.

'I worry that you are too alone, too isolated and too hardened...'

He was, but he couldn't get back, couldn't make himself care about much of anything.

A knock at the library door ten minutes later found him sitting and he pulled his leg down from the ottoman on which it rested.

His butler, Larkin, stood there with yet another message in his hands.

'If it is from Miss Verity Chambers, take it away.'

'It is not, sir. The man who delivered the missive said he came under the instructions of a Mr Twigg from Old Pye Street.'

That had Jasper interested and he held out his hand even as he saw the curiosity of his servant.

'That will be all.'

The message was simple.

The man you be wanting is Viscount Harcourt. He came in to the pub briefly last evening with a friend of his and I recognised the crest on the carriage and asked after his name.

Jasper did not know the fellow at all, but he was suddenly mindful of an invitation he had received ten or so days ago. A colleague he'd known once, Nigel Payne, was to be married to a girl who was Harcourt's niece and had asked Jasper to a celebration party in three days' time. He'd placed the invitation in a drawer, having no intention at all of attending, but now he knew it to be a great opportunity to find out more about Viscount Harcourt.

Another thought came to him forcibly as well. If he asked Miss Charlotte Fairclough to accompany him, she might be able to help. He had promised, after all, to let her know if there were any leads in the case of the missing Harriet White.

A further honesty also struck him. He would like to see the younger Miss Fairclough dressed in a gown of silk and satin, with her hair done and jewellery at her ears and throat. If Meghan could be cajoled to be a chaperon, he was certain Payne would have no objections to the extra guests. The man owed him his life after all.

But would Charlotte Fairclough come? He would visit Howick Place in the morning and make his plans known. If Charlotte was true to form, she would be keen to be a part of the adventure and, if not, then he would go alone.

Lottie was filled with a strange feeling of anticipation as she readied herself for bed.

'You ought not to have been out so late with this cold, Miss Lottie, as it takes nothing in this season for a chest to freshen up into the influenza and then you will be laid low for the whole of the Christmas season, make no mistake about that.'

Claire's chatter filled the background with noise as Lottie thought over her day. She had found Mr Jasper King and lost Harriet White. She'd had word of her brother and had traversed the environs of Old Pye Street with Mr King by her side. Helping her.

Looking in the mirror as Claire brushed out her hair, she saw a face that looked a little bit unfamiliar. Excitement lingered where dullness had been before, a sort of shocking eagerness that brought her alive.

Would he call in again? Would he send a note if Mr Twigg contacted him about Harriet? He had promised Silas's letter, so perhaps that would come? She hoped it would just so that she could see his handwriting and know that it was indeed her brother.

'I have made you a drink of lemon, honey and whisky, miss, and warmed it. It is on your bedside table with a jar of camphor for your chest.'

'Thank you, Claire.'

'I also spoke to Rosa a few hours back near Grey Coat Road and she said you had gone into the streets in search of Harriet White?'

'I did not go alone. Mr King came with me. He was my brother's friend once so he was happy to help our family.'

'Your mother asked me to take good care of you, miss, and I shouldn't be doing my proper duty if I didn't warn you of the dangers of it all. There could be talk…'

An instant tiredness overcame the excitement. 'Talk…?'

'As the daughter of a woman who is both proud and respectable you have to take care. A reputation is an easy thing to lose and a hard one to regain.'

'Meaning…?'

'To be alone for that long with a man at your age and station in life is foolish. I know you to be sensible and prudent, but still…with a man like Mr Jasper King there is the propensity to be persuaded.'

'You know of him?'

'I remember him from years ago, when he used to come to the Foundation with Mister Silas. He were good looking and tall then, but I'm sure that he's even better now for he had that kind of twinkle in his eye that all the girls commented on.'

Well, that had gone, Lottie thought to herself. Now he was largely silent and cross. But that was a lie as well. He was also beautiful and enigmatic and charming and clever. He was kind, too, to his sister and especially to Rosa O'Brian with her slashed cheek.

He had not drawn back or looked away, but had faced her directly and spoken to her as if she was whole and pretty. Lottie knew that Rosa had appreciated the kindness because she would never have got into the carriage with him otherwise.

His limp had seemed to get worse as the hours had passed, the small imbalance a much larger one as they had left Old Pye Street after their sojourn down to the One Tun pub.

She wondered what had happened to have left him

so compromised. But compromised was the wrong word as well. Jasper King's strength was something one could not fail to notice, the pain he so obviously suffered bent to submission by an iron will.

She had to admire such a force.

'Mrs Fairclough and Miss Amelia will be pleased to know that Mister Silas is alive and prospering.' Claire's words came again through her thoughts.

Lottie had wanted to simply pack and take a transport to Lady Malverly's this afternoon when she had first heard the good news about her brother so that her mama and sister could be told of it as soon as possible. But now she tarried.

Perhaps Mr King might come again tomorrow with more news of Harriet and she needed to be here. There was still a good week before she would be expected at the country party and the small window of freedom was welcomed. She had no one to answer to, no one to tell her what to do and how to do it.

This moment brought her a gift of time and independence, and a bequest that she did not want to relinquish before she had to. The hope of it all made her breathless.

'Do you think you might be able to fix my hair tomorrow into that style you so often do for Amelia? The one that is upswept with the ribbons.'

Claire looked perplexed. 'Your hair is completely different from your sister's, Miss Lottie. The curls you have are so much a part of you…'

'I know.' She shook her head and the wildness of her hair was even more pronounced in the candlelight. 'But…' She hardly knew how to formulate her needs. 'It's just sometimes I would like to look more classical.'

'Well, I certainly can try it and perhaps it would suit you. Your nose isn't quite as patrician as your sister's, but your neck is long and slender for all of it. Is Mr King the reason for this change?'

'Oh, I doubt I shall even see him again unless Harriet is somehow miraculously recovered.' She couldn't quite bring herself to tell an outright lie for it was, in truth, because of Jasper that these thoughts had arisen. She wanted to appear more worldly and less…young. She wanted to be more like the beautiful woman who had hung on to his arm at the charity event today and made him look right at her.

So often in her life Lottie had almost felt…invisible. That word made her frown for it was not the sort of magic that conjurors and entertainers wrought on adoring crowds that she ruminated on. No, her invisibility came from the shadows of piety and devotion that left her obscured somehow, buried in the indiscernible goodness of it.

Concentrating on the appearance was shameful and distasteful, she knew this, the greater needs of those vulnerable and defenceless people they helped so much more important. Great pride had false vulgarity attached to it, a petty non-significance allowing one to believe that the outward beauty was far more important than the inward. Mama said so all the time and so had Nanny Beth.

Lottie understood well her own limits of beauty,

but she just suddenly wanted to make the most of what she did have. Her eyes were an unusual colour and, although her nose did not hold the lines fashion now held as desirable, her own turned-up one did not seem untoward on her face. She would have liked to have been taller, but she was curvy. The positives and the negatives formed a list.

She wished she could have just gone to his house and knocked on the door, but she had no idea where it was he resided. Jasper had said that he would send her her brother's letter and this was at least a hope, but Claire's warnings played on her mind, too.

Desperation was probably unattractive and if he wanted to come to see her here he could, without comment, for people dropped in all the time.

She would wait a day or two at the most and if there was no contact whatsoever she would rejoin Mama and Millie.

The very thought of that made her heart sink, though a small sound outside the door had her turning.

'It's just the stray, Miss Lottie, the one who Mr Brown brought in a few days ago. The ugly one. Seems it is in need of company and it's hard to shoo away.'

'I thought that one of the maids said that she might want to take it home.'

'The girl had a mind change, miss, because of its size and now it's stuck here.'

'Let it in then, Claire. It can join me for the night until we sort out its future.'

When the door opened the large dog shot in and sat on the floor beside the bed, its dark eyes upon her. The mongrel was many breeds, Lottie thought, and was an indiscriminate white and brown colour with pointy ears and a long nose.

It looked like a dog who had never fitted in anywhere, but wanted to, for it held the same sort of desperation in its eyes as many of the women who came seeking help from the Foundation did.

She put her hand down and stroked the short bristly fur, surprised to feel the edge of a warm tongue against her skin.

'Good dog,' she said and smiled, ignoring Claire's frown as she took a blanket from the end of her bed and laid it down on the wood for warmth.

'Your mother sneezes all the time in the presence of a dog, Miss Lottie, and will want it gone as soon as she sees it.'

'Then we will have to find it a home quickly.'

As she said this a thought came on the edge of her words. Jasper King might have need of a dog. He had the means to give it a good home and without family he might welcome a companion.

A further consideration complicated the last one. He'd probably insist on a thoroughbred, a dog of lineage and pedigree. In which case she would need to introduce him carefully to this stray, hone him in to the animal's finer points before he only saw the negative. The more she thought about it the more she liked the idea. It would be a way of getting to see Jasper again and of keeping up the connection.

The dog had curled into a ball now and was quietly snoring with a strange rumble of companionship.

After Claire said goodnight Lottie lay there in the moonlight. Overall, it had been a most interesting day. She just prayed that they could find Harriet soon and bring her back to safety.

Chapter Five

Jasper arrived at his sister's home just after ten thirty in the morning and as usual the house was full of noise and movement.

Sarah was sitting on a blanket in the small front parlour, Meghan chasing the toys that she threw in all directions.

'I didn't expect you today?'

He knelt by his niece and said hello which gave him time to formulate exactly what it was he wanted to say.

'I have a situation that needs attending to.'

Meghan's interest looked caught.

'I hadn't told you, but yesterday after I left the party I found Miss Fairclough trudging home through the bad weather alone and so I stopped to offer her a lift back to Howick Place in Westminster.'

'A direction that was the exact opposite to your own?'

He ignored that and went on. 'She was grateful to

be out of the sleet, but on arrival at the Fairclough Foundation a woman ran up to the conveyance to tell us that one of the girls they helped had been reported as missing.'

'Missing?'

'It is thought she may have found herself embroiled in a prostitution ring.'

'God.' Meghan never took the name of the Lord in vain so that gave Jasper some idea as to the magnitude of her shock. 'Did you help look for her?'

He smiled. His sister's kindness was why he was here. She wasn't a person who had much time for social differences and he knew she would not be judgemental.

'Indeed, I did. Miss Fairclough and I went to the area where she was last seen and asked questions. As a result of that we think that she may have got into a carriage with Viscount Harcourt and left town.'

'Harcourt? I have not heard of him.'

'He is having a ball in two days' time here in London and I have an invitation. If I were to take Miss Fairclough with me as my partner for the occasion, would you agree to be her chaperon?'

The wide smile hid other thoughts, but at least she nodded. 'Oh, my goodness, of course I would, Jasper. I would be delighted.' Standing, she swooped up Sarah into her arms. 'Does she have a gown that would suffice for such a ball?'

'I don't know. I had not thought of that.'

'Ask her, then. Will you see her today? If she does

not have one, time will be short, though I cannot see why a dress could not be altered and tailored to fit her and I know just the place to go. This is marvellous…'

Jasper stopped her.

'I am trying to help a woman who may have been kidnapped from Miss Fairclough's family foundation. Do not read anything else into it, Meg.'

'But you are here in London until Christmas, are you not? You won't be leaving till after the Yule season?'

'I won't.'

'Then you have plenty of time to help Miss Fairclough and get to know Sarah.'

Her sister passed over her daughter and Jasper took her, her mouth dribbling all over him and her nose running. Still, she was warm and small and when she simply stilled and cuddled into him he felt a kind of contentment that he had not known for a very long time.

Outside it was beginning to sleet again and inside there was a warm fire and decorations that signified the Christmas season. Meghan adhered to the new custom of cutting a tree and hauling it inside and so the room smelt of pine and the outdoors, the frosted paint his sister had run along the green limbs mimicking snow.

He wished Charlotte Fairclough might have seen such a room, imagining that with her family gone the joy of the season at the Foundation could be much less overt.

He would send a message over to Howick Place to

let her know that he would be visiting in an hour and a half. His eyes went to the large clock on the mantel. It was eleven now. A visitation just after twelve thirty was not too early to be unsettling and, if his sister was right and she had no gown suitable, they would have to get moving to remedy the fact.

'Sarah is growing up right before my eyes, Meg.'

'She is. Stephen wants to try for another child, but…' She stopped.

'But what?' He was astonished when he looked around to see his sister crying.

'It was so difficult trying to conceive Sarah that I don't want to feel like that again. Ever. Besides, my husband barely interacts with her as it is.'

These words came slowly and Jasper could tell that she waited for his answer.

'Perhaps he is worried he might inadvertently hurt her somehow and after so many miscarriages he knows it would break your heart.'

Meghan frowned. 'I had not thought of it like that before.'

'It's because you are a female. Men think differently.'

'I want to be happy. I want us to be a family. I don't want this distance.'

'Then tell him, for I promise he won't know what you are thinking otherwise.'

'I will. Thank you, Jasper, for listening.'

He shook his head. 'You dragged me out of the opium dens and nursed me back to health, Meg. The throes of withdrawal can hardly be easy for anyone to watch and I am grateful.'

'You are my brother.'

A simple truth he smiled at. 'I will always support you, no matter what happens. You know that?'

'I do.' She wiped her face and shook her head. 'But at the moment let us concentrate on the Harcourt ball and in getting Miss Fairclough a dress that will become her.'

He did not push further. Rather he distracted Sarah with a group of small wooden animals that were down on the floor beside him in order to give his sister some time to compose herself.

At exactly half past twelve a stern-looking servant answered the door at the Foundation and brought him through to a small salon down a long, dark corridor. Jasper remembered the place from years ago, his visits to see Silas and the two calls on the older Miss Fairclough coming to mind. A quick glance up the stairwell to the ornate banisters above reassured him that Charlotte was not there, peering down at him, unbidden.

The small annex the Faircloughs used as their private accommodation lay at the back of the Foundation. It was quite a humble dwelling with a sitting room and kitchen and three bedrooms, though there was an attic of sorts at the top.

'If you would wait here, I will find Miss Fairclough.' The man who had answered the door was old and bent over. He wondered if those who worked here had come from straitened circumstances themselves.

Jasper half-hoped that Harriet White had been located and that she was back safe in her job at the laundry. It would be easier that way, less complex. But sometimes what one wished for and what one got were two very different things.

If the girl was still missing, he could go to the Harcourt ball alone and accomplish his tasks of finding out more about the Viscount just as easily as he could if Charlotte Fairclough were with him. The whim of his need to see her foxed him, made him agitated. She would probably be wondering what the hell it was he wanted.

Five minutes later the door opened and she stood there in a plain navy dress with her hair pulled up. Today she looked tired, the dark circles under her eyes noticeable and her dimples nowhere in sight. There was a dog standing next to her, an ugly gangly mongrel who looked him over as he came forward.

'Mr King?' She managed to imbue a question into the two words, a frown crossing her forehead. Her hair had been done in a different style from yesterday, a far fussier style that he thought did not suit her so well. It seemed as if she might have been feeling the same doubt, because her hand wandered up to the back of her neck as if she were trying to pull some of the wayward tendrils across the bareness of skin.

Her dress was different, too, more formal and far darker. It also looked a little big, but the shawl she wore covered quite a bit of it, the redness clashing with the tawny brown of her hair and eyes and making her skin look startlingly white.

'Your letter said you had news of Harriet?'

'I do. Mr Twigg from the One Tun sent over a name. Viscount Harcourt. Is this man familiar to you?'

'He is not. We rarely bump into peers of the realm here.'

Today when she spoke her voice sounded more hoarse than it had yesterday but as yet she had not coughed at all. The smell of camphor had accompanied her in.

The distance between them seemed larger, the ease felt yesterday lost here in the environs of a house that held no trace of the season whatsoever. The fire on the far wall was unlit, lending an unwelcome coldness to the room though the dog sauntered over to stand beside him, its nose pressing into his hand, friendship in the gesture.

A maid had come in with a pot of tea and when she glanced over at him he noticed irritation. Miss Fairclough seemed to pick up on it, too, for as soon as the woman had placed the tray on the table she dismissed her.

'That will be all, Claire.'

'Yes, miss.' A tone of exasperation was prevalent.

He was surprised when Charlotte Fairclough walked over and shut the door, any rules of having a chaperon unobserved entirely.

He did not look happy today, Mr Jasper King with all his certitude and sureness. The way Claire had done her hair was biting into her own confidence, the austere style suiting Millie, but lending a sort of gauche plainness to her own face. Lottie could see in his frown that he preferred the curls. She did, too, but had not had the luxury of time to pull it all down and start over. At least the dog was making gains in forming the acquaintance of Jasper King.

'Please do sit down.' She was glad when he took the chair opposite to her own and smiled when the stray stayed to sprawl out beside him.

'There is to be a ball in two days' time at the home of Viscount Harcourt and I know I will be able to secure three invitations. If my sister stood as a chaperon, might you be willing to accompany me to this occasion and help in the quest to gather information, Miss Fairclough?'

The words were not lightly given, but there was no true heart in them either.

'I realise, of course, that you might indeed have made other plans and I can easily manage alone, but people make their own luck and I thought—'

She interrupted him.

'I would be willing. To help, I mean, as another set of ears and eyes.'

'And you know Miss White. If she were to be somewhere in the house…'

'I could locate her.'

Business and pragmatism. Mr King was a man who did not waste his emotions.

'My sister said that I should also ask if you had a

gown that was suitable for such an occasion. If not, I shall procure one for you.'

'A gown?' Lord, this meeting was getting away from her.

'For the ball. She has contacts.'

'In the fashionable world?'

'Exactly.'

'I am not sure if...'

'If you are worried about the motivations behind such an offer, I hope I can reassure you by saying this is merely a way of helping Miss White. My friend's daughter disappeared five years ago and has never been recovered. I saw what an effect her loss had on him and promised myself if it ever happened again to another I knew I should use the resources I had at my disposal to help and I have plenty of them.'

'I see.'

And she did. The worth of a shilling to a pauper was a fortune and the cost of a gown to a rich man was a fleeting contemplation. Still she was uneasy and knew if Mama ever was to discover the bargain she was making she might not have been happy. Millie was also in the picture. If it was for her betterment that Lottie had sought this whole meeting with Jasper King in the first place, then she certainly was not giving it much importance now.

The guilt of that realisation had her stepping back.

What was she doing? Changing herself entirely for the hope of catching the eye of a man who had made it abundantly clear that he was helping Harriet White for his own personal reasons and that her assistance was required mainly because she could identify Harriet. He would not be interested in her, she was becoming more and more certain of it. Claire had stated the same and Millie had told her years ago that Mr Jasper King was a man who could not settle.

Which meant her sister might have tried to make it happen. Which also meant that she had liked him a lot more than she had ever let on.

Lottie felt scattered and a little afraid, the directions her mind and body were taking her so very unknown. Should she allow Jasper to talk her into this scheme of his, or should she cry off and rejoin her sister and her mama in the country, knowing that she might have just had a lucky escape?

Still, if Harriet should disappear for ever like the daughter of his friend, guilt would be on her conscience as the one who had turned down a man who could have made the only difference in locating her. Surely she had to at least try?

Today Jasper's beauty had morphed into menace, the soft velvet in his eyes taking on a harder glint. Not an easy man, not a tame one either. His honesty held sharp edges and hidden truths.

Gilbert Griffiths, for all his shortcomings, cared for the vulnerable and would make it his lifetime's work to seek the betterment of those who could not manage it themselves. Jasper had his own agenda. She imagined he barely saw the need on the streets of London town or the souls lost to the vices of extreme poverty.

Her father would have said Mr King was a toff,

a man raised in money and who saw the collection of more and more of it as his God. He'd admitted he was rich. He'd also said that people made their own luck. How condescending was that?

But then Jasper had never seen Patricia Harris and her three children in the backstreets of the Rookery with asthma sucking the very breath from her lungs and a husband who spent every spare farthing down at the local tavern. Or Peter Bailey with his legs lost in an accident in the Perkins Rents and crawling in the filth to beg for alms, his wife at home, bedridden. Or little Katie Burrows left with her aged grandparents when her mother and father and two siblings had been taken away on a single night from the influenza last winter.

Harriet White was only one of a thousand young women who had been lured by the promise of riches and trodden the road to ruin in the hope of it. Women who would do so again and again and again, not because they were immoral, but because they had small children to feed or a roof was needed over their heads to keep their families alive and safe.

This was the truth of life at the Foundation, the truth of living here on the edge of the Irish Rookery. It was the truth of striving for something more than the easier option of simply giving up.

A turn under the sheets held value and who had the right to judge whether or not such an exchange was sensible business practice? All Lottie did know was that it should be a choice, everybody's personal pathway, and she doubted that Harriet White had ever been given hers.

The clock in the corner struck the half-hour. The tea on the table had lost its steam. The sounds outside her windows dimmed in the wind and the house breathed in to see just what she might say.

'If your sister were to help me find a suitable gown, when might I expect her to call upon me?'

'This afternoon around three.' The answer came back immediately. 'Meghan will take you to her own seamstress, I expect, for a fitting.'

'I shall agree to what you suggest only on the proviso that when my brother returns from the Americas with his newly made fortune, then you must allow me to pay you back every penny of your expenditure. I do not wish to feel indebted.'

The smile he gave her harked back a little to yesterday's meeting.

'Very well, Miss Fairclough.'

He rifled in his jacket pocket then and brought out a letter. Silas's letter. She saw his handwriting on the missive.

'I promised you this. I hope it helps.'

At that he stood and bowed in the manner of one born to the social mores of the wealthy. The dog stood with him as if it, too, might follow and she saw Mr King's frown as he realised the exact same thing.

'What's his name?'

'We are not sure. He was found as a stray and is looking for a home.'

'He seems friendly.'

'He is also clean and quiet.' Then Lottie thought of his snoring in the night and flushed. 'But he is a large dog who would need an owner with the means available to feed him.'

The silence lengthened between them and then he was gone. The space he left seemed so much dimmer than it had been, the vital and mercurial Mr King leaving a void in his wake and a silence that was deafening.

Lottie held on to the letter he had delivered like a lifeline, perusing the contents before folding it again and placing it into her pocket. When Claire returned to collect the tea tray her frown told Lottie exactly what it was she thought of Jasper's latest visitation.

'I am glad at least that he did not stay long.' Her maid announced this as she trounced out, carefully leaving the door ajar.

After she had left Lottie extracted the correspondence again and sat to read at her leisure. The handwriting was as familiar as the message.

Richard Jackson, a man Silas had mentioned before in other letters, and her brother were about to sign off for a large stake in a new railway company on the eastern coast of America.

Her heart sank. This sort of optimism was so true of her brother, for she remembered other times he had sent word of wildly successful schemes that had faltered at the last minute.

'Please God let this one come to something,' she whispered, for the date on the top was the sixth of September, over three months ago.

She could see why he had written to Mr King, though, for there was a large passage about the technical capabilities of different railway line gauges. She wondered how he had answered all the queries and resolved to ask the next time she saw him. But for now she folded the letter again and held it close to her heart.

At least she'd had word that Silas was safe and well and that was more important to her than any dubious fortune. She also hoped the stray dog had made a favourable impression on Mr Jasper King.

Jasper went straight to his club and ordered a stiff brandy, refusing the offer of a cheroot from the footman who waited upon him. His leg ached and his body quivered with the frustration of his last encounter with the impossible Miss Fairclough, for he felt that what he had said had been taken by her in exactly the wrong way.

God. He was usually so much more in charge of situations and so much less in doubt about the outcomes. She made him query everything. His motives. His honesty. His commitment.

The trouble was she changed every time he met her. Yesterday she had seemed vulnerable. Today she had not. Yesterday her curls were a wild halo about her head. Today they were scrimped and scraped back, the pins visible all along the line of her hair.

Today when the shawl had slipped he had seen the flesh of her bosom over the plunging neck on her bodice, the blue of her veins just beneath her skin raised in the cold. He noticed, too, that the pulse of her heart in her throat had risen every time he had stepped nearer.

Was she afraid of him? Did she imagine he might hurt her? The lemon and lavender scent was also muted, a more pungent musky floral warring with the cleaner bouquet. The camphor was there, too.

Nigel Payne stepped across into his view unexpectedly and took a seat opposite him.

'My God, it is so good to see you, Jasper. Can I get you something to drink?'

He raised his glass. 'No, I have enough for now. I'm home for Christmas, but will leave for Manchester in the first week of January.'

'Another new venture? Once I thought perhaps you might never…' He left the sentence hanging and Jasper took it up again.

'My leg is much better now. It rarely pains me.' Even he could hear the flatness of deceit in his answer, but it was all that was left to him now.

Relief filled Nigel's eyes. 'I hope that you have received my invitation to a ball on the twelfth to meet my bride-to-be. I had not heard back from you?'

'I am sorry. Yes, I would like to come, but is it possible to bring my sister and a friend as well?'

'Of course, Jasper. You, after all, are the true reason I am still in the world in the first place.'

'Hardly.' He didn't want to speak of such a thing, didn't want to remember, didn't want a rehash of the whole incident.

As if understanding his reticence Nigel moved

on. 'You were always diplomatic, Jasper. And clever. I hear you have scorched a trail through the stolid world of civil engineering with your ideas and your billowing worth has those in your shadow talking. Silas Fairclough has been making waves, too, it is said.'

Now this caught his attention. 'You know him?'

'Through his sister Amelia. The younger daughter Charlotte was the one I had always hoped to know better, but she made it abundantly clear that she held no interest in doing the same.'

'When was this?'

'Oh, a year or so back. But then everyone loves Lottie, though she never takes the time to realise it. By the expression on your face I see that you, too, have met her?'

'Briefly.' Jasper schooled in his thoughts and changed the subject. 'Who is it that you have the pleasure of making Mrs Nigel Payne?'

'Miss Eloise Proctor. A girl from Cheshire whose family is an old one from those parts. They breed horses.'

'She sounds stellar.'

'She is sensible, wealthy, passably good looking and has the sort of hips to easily provide heirs. In short, every requirement I am looking for.'

Such a list made Jasper frown. Were he to ever note his requirements in a wife he imagined it would include none of the above, save sense perhaps.

'Her uncle is Viscount Harcourt.'

Payne had always been a man who dropped names

into conversations and for this one moment Jasper was glad of it.

'I do not know him. What is he like?'

'Wealthy, energetic, slightly mad, I think, but very charming with it.'

'Is he married?'

'No, and he never has been. He has a plethora of young women who follow him around like lapdogs, but no one permanent. Perhaps he enjoys just playing the field. I know for sure that money flows through his hands like water.'

'Could you introduce him to me at your ball?'

'Of course.'

Their talk then turned to the projects Jasper had been involved in across the past years and it was another hour before he could get away and make for home.

Once at his town house in Piccadilly he helped himself to a further brandy and sat in his library before a roaring fire to read.

He wondered how his sister's appointment with Charlotte Fairclough this afternoon had gone. Had the dressmaker had some luck in fitting a gown that would be sufficient? He had resisted calling in on his way home mainly because he knew Meghan would make a meal over such a thing. Already she was looking at him with sideways glances. To encourage more would be foolishness.

He remembered the conversation with Nigel Payne and the list of attributes he had attached to his wife-to-be. If he were ever to be married, which he highly doubted, what would his own list look like?

Joy was the first word that came unbidden. He needed joy to fill up his lonely life. Someone who laughed a lot and helped people. A woman who was beautiful in her own way. Curly hair and whisky-coloured eyes leapt into the mix, shocking him.

'God.' He swallowed the brandy and put away the decanter so that he would not reach for more. His vices now were tightly controlled things, each one let out only for intermittent moments lest he be persuaded by the darkness to step back in.

He wouldn't sleep well tonight because the pain in his leg was building and he already felt sick from it. No one position eased it for long so he simply gave up and stood watching the moon through scudding clouds, the lights of London sprawled before him.

He remembered the moment it had happened, the sheared-off link pin falling from its shackle.

He'd taken the thrust of steel himself, the sharp edges ripping across muscle and bone. If he shut his eyes, he could recall the exactness of the agony. Its echo was still there inside him, calling for relief.

Kindness. He wanted that in a wife. And an ability to see him as the man he once had been despite the scars. A sense of adventure would be welcome and a companion to talk to him about the books he read and the music he listened to. *Morality.* A woman who would stick to her word in hardship as well as in ease. *Softness.* A body to hold in the very black of night when memories demanded an audience.

Love. He could not expect that of her, but liking would be enough. Abiding his touch, understanding his limitations, seeing in the man he was now the one he had been and guiding him back into the light.

A long and impossible list. Better to stay single because there was no way he could fulfil any reciprocal expectations. Anger and regret beat through his blood like a drum and he could hardly stop it.

He would be a poor mate for the woman he had conjured up with his foolish and detailed list. A spoiled and blemished groom. He leaned back against the wall to one side of the window and raised his leg, the muscles jumping in protest. Stretch and release. Stretch and release. The nerves burned with such a movement and he took in a breath, feeling the sweat begin to build in the folds of his skin and the heat rising up to claim him.

Another moment and he would be down. On the floor, unable to carry his body weight, and there he would lie until the dawn when the spasms would finally lessen, the rigours of agony allowing living once again.

A very good sleeper. A new thought for the list. He did not wish for his would-be wife to ever see this side of his deformity and torment because he knew then he would also see pity.

A woman who would not gossip. A woman who wanted children. A woman who might take him to her bed without flinching.

A new crescendo of agony. He held in his breath and felt his heartbeat accelerate.

A woman who smelt nice. A woman who spoke well. A woman who might pretend that he was a whole man still.

He lost consciousness just as the mantel clock struck one, the wind outside howling through the bare limbs of the English oaks in Green Park opposite.

Chapter Six

Charlotte Fairclough's hair today was curly again and his sister looked more than animated. Meghan had sent a message asking for him to meet them at the teashop on the corner of Kensington Road and it was with trepidation he made the journey.

He felt hollowed out and exhausted after his night, but at least his thigh was back in some sort of a working order and with a bath and a shave he was ready again to meet the world.

'I hoped you would come, Jasper. I said to Charlotte you are prone to doing your own thing and I was not sure that you would even be here. We have so much to tell you, though, and all of it is good news.'

Charlotte listened with the same sort of silence he often employed when subjected to his sister's verbosity, but she was smiling and the gold gown she had on was the same one she had worn to the charity event the day before yesterday. It matched her eyes and her hair and brought out the colour of her skin.

'Meghan has been most kind to me, Mr King, and very patient, for in truth the time it takes to alter a gown is a long one. The seamstress was competent, however, and I learnt a lot from watching her.'

'You sew?'

'I do,' she returned and gestured to the fabric of her skirt. 'Mama and I made this dress just a short while ago. My sister Amelia has the very same pattern, but her gown is in a vibrant green, which suits her eyes admirably.'

'I remember you speaking of Miss Amelia Fairclough years ago, Jasper.' Meghan joined in on the conversation now.

He tried to smile, but felt that the tightness of the effort failed him somewhat. 'I knew her only for a short while.'

His sister sat forward then, observing him intently. 'You look tired.' His spirits sank. This was exactly why he had not wanted to come today.

'I am fine.'

'My brother had an accident a few years back and damaged his leg. It pains him sometimes.' Meghan was explaining this to Charlotte when the waiter arrived, which broke into her unwanted account. Jasper was glad for the interruption.

'A coffee, please.'

Charlotte asked for tea and so did his sister.

'We have some news of Viscount Harcourt,' Charlotte stated quietly, making sure her voice could not be overheard. 'There was another woman in the dressmaker's salon who is also to attend the Harcourt ball.

She was adamant that the Viscount had retired to the country and would only be back in London for a little time. Perhaps he has taken Harriet there, to his estate?'

Jasper had no idea in which county that would be, but as if sensing his perplexity his sister supplied the answer.

'His estate is near Bromley, in Kent, Jasper, which is only forty minutes from London.'

'Convenient.'

'Very, though I imagine that the Viscount is in the city now as the function is tomorrow night.'

He was grateful for the coffee that had materialised. A ball was the very last thing he needed given the recent agony of his leg, but he could not avoid it now.

He wanted to ask Charlotte Fairclough to wear her hair down in exactly the style she was sporting at that moment, twists of wild curls escaping from their anchor at the back of her head. He hoped she might choose a dress, too, that would show off something of her body. But of course he said nothing. Meghan had always had an eye for what suited her and he could only pray that would translate into her choice for Charlotte.

Besides, his sister's wicked smile when she glanced across at him made him cagey.

Jasper looked pale today and wary. When Meghan had asked him of it he had bitten back quickly.

Could his injury be worse than she imagined? Was

there another problem that was underlying the accident's repercussions?

She was pleased to see him and she wished his sister might suddenly remember she had some important thing to do and leave them alone for at least a few moments. But of course she did not because there were rules that society adhered to and leaving an unmarried woman alone in the company of an unmarried man in a public place would have been shocking.

'Did you send word to your mother about your brother's letter, Miss Fairclough?' He addressed her directly.

'Not yet, Mr King. I felt it prudent to wait to see if there was any good news regarding Harriet. Then I could send both tidings together.'

In truth, she had not wished to convey her thoughts to the country just yet in case her mother should see Harriet's disappearance as a reason to cut short her visit and return to the Foundation. Lilian was always insistent on knowing any problems at all that occurred with the girls she helped and Lottie swallowed away guilt, but kept to her path.

She wanted a few days without the interruption of her family in the company of Mr King and she longed to go to the ball. Like Cinderella, she thought, dressed in her finery.

The gown that Jasper had paid for was stunning. It was the most beautiful dress she had ever worn and ever would wear. A mid-blue cloth spun from silk and wreathed in lace which had fitted her like a glove once it had been altered. Lottie wished Millie could have been there, too, getting fitted for a dress of her own. Another cloud of guilt settled, but tomorrow night she was going to a ball with the most handsome man in all of London and she was going to enjoy it.

As a result of her thoughts she smiled at him and he smiled back, the dark in his eyes lightening a little and the mood brighter.

She knew a few of the most popular dances. Would Jasper ask her to be his partner? She imagined a waltz and the closeness that was a part of it. Shocking. Scandalous. Appealing and enticing.

As if he had read her thoughts he began to speak.

'I am sure you will be the belle of the ball, Miss Fairclough. Do you dance?'

She hated the blush that rose from his words and wondered for a second if they were not facetious, but he did not look like he teased and so she answered in the same vein.

'A little. Mama taught Millie and me at home some-times during the long winter nights. I doubt I have any finesse though and certainly I have no practice.'

'I met Mr Nigel Payne in town yesterday and he asked to be remembered to you.'

This time there was a definite twinkle in his eyes.

What could Nigel Payne have told him? He had courted her briefly and ardently a year or so ago, but she had never encouraged it.

'He is to be married to the niece of Viscount Harcourt and he said he would introduce us to the man.'

'Wasn't Nigel Payne the man who—?'

Jasper cut his sister off and shook his head.

Secrets, thought Lottie. More and more of them. An awkward silence followed until Jasper dredged up a new topic.

'Payne told me that he keeps a list of what he most wants in a wife. His bride-to-be fits each criterion.'

'Such as what?' Meghan was laughing now, her interest piqued, but her brother was not being drawn into the gossip.

'I cannot remember, but I wish him well. He deserves some happiness.'

Again the undercurrent played quietly beneath what was said. Had there been bad blood between Jasper King and Mr Payne? Lottie could not imagine Mr Payne to be deceitful or truly evil. If anything, he was lightweight and fairly shallow.

He had pleaded for her hand in marriage until Lottie could bear it no more and told him that she felt nothing for him save a friendship. She should have been kinder, but by that point all she wanted was for him was to be gone. She remembered her mother saying that she worried no man would ever live up to the standards Lottie seemed to require, a barb that had hurt at the time. But she'd felt no sense of heat or excitement and her reading had led her to believe things like that were important.

When the bells of a local church peeled out in the early afternoon Jasper King stood and replaced his hat.

'I shall pick you both up tomorrow night at eight in my carriage. Will that give you enough time to get ready?'

'It will.' Meghan leaned across and kissed his

cheek and Lottie smiled at such closeness between them, for Jasper King looked as if he needed a friend.

A brief tip of the head and he was away, a tall and rangy man dressed today almost completely in black. She saw his carriage and horses standing waiting at the corner, a man of means and importance.

'He used to be happier and I wish he would be so again.' Meghan's words drifted over, but Lottie did not ask how, reasoning that it was his business and he would not want her to pry.

It was the day of the ball and Jasper would already be on his way to take them to it.

Lottie peered at herself in the long mirror in front of her. This upstairs chamber at Meghan Gibson's house in Kensington was decorated in deep browns and sported a sofa that was the colour of emeralds. It was one of the prettiest rooms Lottie had ever been in.

A maid had been dispatched to help her with her hair and tonight she had it loosely fastened at her nape, a series of curls sweeping across her shoulders and down her back. An artful style that suited the line of the dress.

The bodice of mid-blue fell off her shoulders, a ruched band crossing at her breasts and falling to a low and pointed waist. Below that the bell-shaped skirt draped into thick folds and when she walked the silk swished in a way that felt foreign and fascinating. On her feet she wore embroidered slippers and the whole ensemble was to be protected from the weather by a high-collared thick woollen cloak.

Jasper's sister had made no demands of the dress-maker to save money, but had gone ahead in a flourish and picked out the most highly priced garments in the shop. Expensive and classical, for if there was one thing Lottie had discovered it was that Meghan Gibson held excellent taste in everything she chose.

The maid who'd been fussing around her finally stood back, looking pleased. 'The mistress always did have an eye for what suits people and this gown most certainly looks well on you, Miss Charlotte.'

Claire, in one corner folding away the bath things, also glanced over with a smile. She was far happier this evening, caught up with the excitement of getting ready and more than willing to learn the art of dressing a lady's hair from the more experienced Gibson servant.

Jasper's sister looked stunning, her gown a deep green which suited the dark of her hair, the fabric falling across her body like watered silk. Lottie felt indebted to her for not only had she been helpful but she had also been very kind and nothing seemed too much trouble to ensure her chosen outfit was exactly the way Meghan imagined it. Lottie knew if the whole choice of what to wear had been left to her she would never have made such a fine job of it.

Five moments later they were both standing down-stairs in a room with a roaring fire, Meghan's husband with them as they waited for Mr King to arrive.

Mr Stephen Gibson was a thickset man, his hair balding and his height hardly imposing. He was not an easy man either, Lottie thought, his next words making her frown.

'Don't let Harcourt anywhere near you, Meghan, for there are some less-than-salubrious rumours about him.'

'Rumours?' Meghan sounded interested.

'He hangs around with a fairly fast crowd, it is said. Personally, I shouldn't want him as a friend.'

As he spoke the door opened and Jasper came into the room. If Lottie had thought him beautiful before, then tonight he surpassed every expectation. He looked dark and dangerous, the deep tones of his clothing emphasising this, the only brightness apparent being a white shirt beneath his coat and waistcoat. Even his neck tie was sombre.

'Ladies.' He bowed quietly and then acknowledged Meghan's husband before his glance came back to Charlotte, the scorching gaze taking in her blue gown and hairstyle.

'Miss Fairclough, I see my sister has not failed in her quest to clothe you.'

'She has been most generous, though I hope I do such a wonderful gown justice.' Her words sounded squeezed and hollow. She could barely breathe under such a close and sensual perusal.

'Rather more than that, I think. Could you keep one dance on your card for me? A slow one. Perhaps the waltz?'

She'd hoped he might have asked for more than a single turn, but of course his leg restricted him.

'I should be honoured, Mr King.' Lottie imagined

his arms around her and the distance between them closed. She wished that she had paid a little more attention to the detail of the dance steps Lilian had tried to instil into them, lessons where Millie had always been the star pupil while she could barely wait for them to end.

It was what she did, Lottie thought, began things and then never finished them off quite properly, the next idea catching her attention and then the next.

Mama despaired of her sometimes, she knew that she did, for she had once overheard her speaking to Nanny Beth.

'Lottie will never stop searching. She is so like Henry sometimes, passionate and busy and impatient for change. It worries me this restlessness.'

Nanny Beth had taken some time in answering, but Lottie had stood there, waiting to hear what she might say.

'Given time and space Lottie will find her potential in one of the endless possibilities of life, Lilian. Stop worrying and just wait and see.'

How she had loved that answer!

Well, tonight was one of those endless possibilities of life. She had never had a dress quite like this one. She had never had her hair fashioned so expertly. She had never been squired to a social occasion by a man as magnificent as Jasper King. And on top of all that was the chance of finding Harriet. How she prayed that this might come true and that they could then just simply bundle her lost friend into the carriage and bring her back to safety.

* * *

Miss Charlotte Fairclough had transformed from a very pretty young woman into a breathtakingly beautiful one. Jasper could hardly take it in, the blue gown wrapped about her in a way that showed off her figure and caught at the golden lights in her hair. He could not believe that he had asked her to save a waltz for him. God, he never danced at these things and his leg was still smarting from another poor night's sleep. He could see his sister's surprise, too, at his offer of a dance and cursed his carelessness anew.

Once he had enjoyed dancing, and running and walking for miles through the countryside. Such exercise had been an outlet for the stress of his busy job and a way to relax. But all that had changed in a second when the pin on the coupling had broken and the casing of the carriage had dragged across his thigh, leaving him sedentary and frustrated and reliant on a stick. At least he had finally got rid of that monstrosity, though he kept it still in his wardrobe, a silver-balled mahogany reminder of how far he had come.

'Will it be crowded tonight, do you think, at the Harcourts?' Meghan asked this as she took a glass of brandy handed to her by Stephen. Jasper was glad to receive his own to help quieten his astonished appreciation of Charlotte Fairclough.

'Great wealth often brings out those who hope for a slice of the same, but it won't hinder us. All we need are the contacts he keeps and the hope of a misplaced word or two. I am relying on the fact that he is a braggart.'

'So you do not think Harriet will be there?' Charlotte's query held trepidation.

'I hardly think a young girl who is his mistress would be welcome at a society event, but she could be somewhere in the house.'

'He's a known philanderer, Jasper, and the family have almost wiped their hands of him.' Stephen said this. 'Such antics might have been dismissed in a younger man, but Harcourt is coming up to forty and there are no heirs for the title.'

'Which means two things. The first is that he needs to marry well and the second is that Harriet White will not be a likely candidate.'

Jasper wished he could have stated that differently, but Charlotte was a woman who had seen the harsher sides of life in the Foundation and would understand the implications of ruin as few others her age would have been able to. Her next words emphasised this.

'I am certain she would know that. She is not a stupid girl which is why I think she was in that carriage against her will. She would realise the dangers of throwing her lot in with a man who could offer her nothing and leaving a job at the laundry that was a secure one.'

'Well then, let us truly hope we find out something useful tonight.' Meghan finished her brandy and turned to her husband. 'I doubt we will be very late.'

Stephen shook his head. 'Take your time for I have a meeting to attend in the city. I hope you enjoy yourself.'

'I will, as it is not every day that my brother asks me to a ball.'

Outside their carriage waited at the kerb and Jasper held out his hand to Charlotte. Seeing her slight hesitation, he waited.

'It's a high climb in all your finery, Miss Fairclough.'

She placed her gloved hand in his and when her fingers curled across his own, a bolt of shock raced through him. He could not remember ever feeling this sort of reaction before with any woman and the surprise kept him wordless. He drew away his grasp as soon as she was safely in and deliberately did not look to see if she had felt what he had. Once Meghan was in he came up the steps to take a place beside his sister which meant that although he was not touching Charlotte he was directly opposite her. Her face was shadowed in the dusk and she sat very still, even her fingers clasped in her lap unmoving.

The thought came next that he seldom saw the younger Miss Fairclough in such immobility as she was always bustling here and there. He hoped she was not nervous about finding Harriet White and he also hoped that she would not feel out of place at a society ball.

She looked small and lost somehow, the finery emphasising her beauty, but taking away the spirit of her adventurousness. He wondered how much she could actually see without her pair of spectacles and he wished his sister had procured jewellery for her as her slender neck looked awfully bare.

Her heart was racing so fast Lottie thought she might simply fall over and so she sat, drawing inward to try to find a calm that had fled when Jasper had taken her hand.

Even through the fabric of her gloves she had known his warmth and his strength, the astonishment of his touch frightening. She was knocked off balance, all steadiness dissipated under the promise of what might come next and as they travelled she chanced a glance at him, his face in darkness illuminated momentarily by the gaslights in the street. He looked indifferent, aloof and unconcerned, all the things that she did not feel.

She knew Meghan had seen her anguish because she was now smiling at her with worry in her eyes as she squeezed her hand.

'It won't be as daunting as you think, Charlotte. With the crush of the ball and the copious amounts of drink taken it's more likely to be an entertainment that is a little distant. Like the theatre or a puppet show. When all else fails I find a smile covers every social situation whether it be a large or a small gathering.'

Her brother gave the impression that he didn't quite agree, but when Lottie caught his eyes he glanced away and did not look back.

Let them think the ball was what had her upset. It was an easier truth than the one that beat inside of her.

She would never fit into the world of Jasper King.

No matter how much she might have wanted to.

Her father was the impoverished fourth son of an earl and her mama had risen up through the working classes into the world of trade. The Faircloughs owned very little, for the currency they mostly dealt in was that of dreams. The dream of helping those down on their luck, the dream of tutorship and self-improvement. A dream of financial security for people who had never known it.

Taking in a breath, she admonished herself for even considering the thought that there could be something between Mr King and herself. He was helping her find Harriet and after that he would be off again into the realm of his successful civil engineering company, establishing the railways. His family was far grander than hers had ever been and he moved in the higher circles of society with ease. Meghan had told her he owned a town house in Piccadilly and other property in Liverpool and by his own account he had plenty of resources at hand. Enough to buy her family out ten times over probably. Enough to find a wife who could bring the same largesse into a marriage should he desire it. The realisation reminded her that she had begun all of this in order to reintroduce him to her sister, but had hardly given that a thought today.

The ridiculousness of her own hopes crashed down upon her and even in the new dress with her hair done she felt sad. There would be no fairy-tale ending for her, no splendid and glorious transformation into a woman whom Jasper might truly find attractive. Yet he was helping her and for that she owed him her eternal gratitude. It was enough. It was more than enough. Fixing a smile on her lips, she looked out of the window as the façade of an impressive town house came into sight.

* * *

Everything shone. The room, the people, the music and the lights above. It was as though she had crossed the threshold of ordinary and arrived at another place entirely, a place where money held no matter, the everyday struggles of most of the population of London consigned here to the forgotten.

'My father would be turning in his grave to see the waste of so much money.'

Jasper next to her looked down. 'The Viscount is a hedonist and a shallow one at that. I doubt whether your father would have ever given him a thought.'

Such words were surprising. 'You knew my papa?'

'Vaguely. I was saddened by Henry's premature death.'

'As were we all. It was a love match for my parents. They saw each other and fell in love in a second. Just like that.'

'Like a story?' There was a note in his voice which denoted disbelief.

'Sometimes fairy tales do come true, Mr King. There have been many at the Foundation who find lives they never before felt were possible. Harriet was such a one and she was thrilled when she obtained permanent employment in the laundry.'

He acknowledged such an outcome and they came on to the end of a long line of people.

'It's a receiving line.' He sounded impatient.

'Just smile.' Meghan had caught them up now, having been waylaid by a friend she had seen as she stepped down from the carriage. 'Remember to address Harcourt with "my lord" if he asks you any questions, Charlotte, as he looks like the sort of man who expects to be deferred to.'

'A popinjay,' Jasper added. 'God help us all.'

Nigel Payne came to stand beside them and he was as effusive as Lottie remembered him to be as he grabbed her hand.

'Miss Fairclough.' He bent down to kiss her knuckles and she resisted the urge to pull away. 'I'd heard that you would be coming tonight and it is a rare treat to see you so very radiant. Are your mama and sister with you?'

'No, they are in the country, Mr Payne, for the Christmas season.'

'Well, let me introduce you personally to Lord Harcourt. I'm to be married, you see, later in the year to his niece, so it's a close relationship.'

She felt Jasper beside her breathe out hard.

'Did Mr King tell you how he saved my life? No, I see he did not so I shall make it a point to relate the incident to you later. Mrs Gibson.' He had suddenly sighted Meghan. 'Two of the most beautiful women in the room with one man. Well, that hardly seems fair, but then your brother always did attract the most splendid of girls.'

'Which one is Harcourt?' Jasper broke in now, giving Lottie the impression he had lost patience with such rambling nonsense.

'There.' Mr Payne gestured to a tall man a few yards away, a man dressed in a colourful silk waistcoat and a deep navy satin coat.

He looked like someone who placed great stock in his looks. On the fingers of the hand he held out to those in welcome he wore a number of rings, each one more gaudy than the one next to it.

As their names were announced Viscount Harcourt looked towards them.

'Ah, Mr King, thank you for coming for I have heard much about your adventures to the north with the railways. My niece's husband-to-be also sings your praises.' His eyes then registered Lottie at Jasper's side and he took her cold hand in his warm one. 'Miss Charlotte Fairclough of the Fairclough Foundation, I understand. It is a pleasure to meet you.' Letting go of Lottie's fingers, he tipped his head to Meghan. 'Mrs Gibson.'

The fact that she hailed from the Foundation didn't seem to disturb Harcourt unduly. This fact set up a further question, for had Harriet wished to escape the clutches of Viscount Harcourt the powerful force of the Fairclough Foundation should have been worrying to a man who had simply taken what he wanted. Jasper seemed to have surmised exactly the same thing because he moved straight on to another topic.

'Your ball has all the makings of an unmitigated success, Viscount Harcourt.'

Harcourt laughed, clearly pleased by the compliment.

'Wait until you see the entertainment I have planned. Such a divergence from the more normal etiquette should prove most interesting.'

Lottie could see that Jasper was astonished. Perhaps society balls were usually more plain occasions, then? Given that she had never once attended one she had no idea whatsoever.

'There's a gambling room, too, where I can promise the stakes will be hefty. I know such things in this climate are frowned upon, but I remember a time when they were not. I dare say you might, too, Mr King?'

'I do, my lord.' The words sounded forced. 'You have thought of everything.'

Then they moved on to the introductions with other family members. Mr Payne's bride-to-be, Eloise Proctor, was a surprise in that she was a large girl with kind eyes. Of all those here in the line she was the one to whom Lottie warmed the most.

She was glad when the introductions were finished and they came to a staircase leading down into a crowded room.

'This is where our work begins,' Jasper said quietly, 'for someone here might know something about Harriet White and, as soon as Harcourt joins the throng, we will aim to get as close to him as we can.'

'You think he will talk of her?'

'Oh, there's a strong possibility. He will be elated by his successful gathering and wine will loosen his tongue further.'

Lottie remembered a quote she knew. *'"I say the gentleman had drunk himself out of his five senses."'*

'Shakespeare?' Jasper's query about the origin of her words held humour.

'*The Merry Wives of Windsor.* My mother loves his plays.'

'Do you read widely, Miss Fairclough?'

'I do indeed, Mr King. I like adventure stories and books about far-off places.'

His frown worried her, but Meghan had caught their attention now with her notice of a group of young girls to one side.

'Is your Harriet one of those ladies, Charlotte?'

'No, unfortunately she is not.'

A breathtakingly beautiful woman had suddenly materialised at their side, the same blonde guest from the charity event the other day accompanying her.

'Jasper?' Her plea held great emotion and Lottie thought just for a moment that the newcomer might well break down into tears.

'Mrs Alworthy.'

'Verity, please. Surely we have not come to be quite that distanced?' Her voice was tremulous and desperate.

Jasper turned towards her. 'Allow me to introduce Miss Charlotte Fairclough. Charlotte, this is Mrs Verity Alworthy.'

A slight hesitancy followed.

'I hoped I might have a few moments to speak to you, Jasper. Alone?'

She seemed fragile. She was also looking at Mr King as if he were the answer to all her prayers.

Lottie thought Jasper might simply refuse her, but then he demurred, leaving Meghan and her in the company of the other woman.

'I do hope he shan't be too long,' Meghan said and looked at the dance floor with longing.

'It seems as if dancing is the least important of things, Mrs Gibson. My friend Verity's heart has been broken.'

'Perhaps then, Miss Seymour, she ought to have thought of that when she left my brother perfunctorily on the eve of their nuptials.'

There was a note in Meghan's voice that Lottie had not heard there before. A challenge and a direct protection of her sibling. She certainly did not look as if she liked either of these newcomers.

Sensing opposition, the other woman backed down.

'Your cough seems a lot better tonight, Miss Fairclough?'

'It is, thank you. I procured some special medicine from an herbalist in Rochester Row on the edge of the Irish Rookery and it seems to be doing the trick.'

A look of disdain passed into the other woman's eyes. 'I forget your Foundation lies so close to that part of town.'

'We provide services to the population there, so it is entirely well placed.'

The conversation faltered.

When Jasper and Mrs Verity Alworthy returned to them Mrs Alworthy did not look at all pleased. As the orchestra struck up in preparation for the waltz he took Charlotte's arm, withdrawing himself from the whole situation.

On the dance floor he faced her directly. 'I am

sorry. Mrs Alworthy is an old acquaintance who has problems.'

So he would not say anything of the relationship between them? Meghan's words echoed in her brain.

Why had Verity Alworthy left him? What had he thought at the time? The eve of a marriage sounded like particularly poor timing to leave anyone in the lurch. Lottie wondered how that had played out.

Certainly now Jasper looked angry at the other woman's interruption. She also sensed guilt.

He was not a man who was easy to read and she knew that there were things about him that were hidden. Women liked him. She could see in those around him their stares and hopeful glances. Lottie thought that had she been Verity Alworthy, on the cusp of becoming Mrs Jasper King, she would have fought tooth and nail to keep him.

'She is upset?'

'She has fairly recently lost a husband.'

The words sounded rough, a flare of fury threaded through them. When he moved into the dance she felt his right side lurch and his arms tighten. Then he seemed to recover, his grip loosening.

'It's been a while since I have done this.'

She frowned as the dark in his eyes raked across her, the loss there so at odds with all he showed the world.

'I am not a proficient dance partner, Mr King. My own style is the result of a few practised hours at home with my sister and brother. I can claim no finesse whatsoever.'

He laughed and a warmth spread through her, her hand curling across his nape, bringing him in. Instinctive. Shocking. It was as if it was only Jasper and her alone on this dance floor, the rest of the ball falling away somehow into nothingness.

She felt his body against her, felt the rhythm of the music and the play of light, the rise and fall of movement smooth even given his limp. Two halves, both made more as a whole.

'I think you are well practised, Mr King, despite your protesting otherwise.'

To one side she could see Verity Alworthy staring at them with a heavy frown on her beautiful face.

'I was supposed to marry her.'

The words said out loud and with the woman present were a shock to her.

'But you did not?'

'I got injured. The timings were unfortunate.' He brushed off her concern and asked a question of his own.

'What do you make of Nigel Payne?'

'He is a man who needs a woman and I like the girl who will become his bride. She seems kind.'

'You were not interested in his advances?'

'He told you of his attentions?' She shook her head. 'I value my freedom, Mr King, and I am sure I must have related such to him on numerous occasions.'

He'd asked Charlotte to dance in order to get away from Verity, but now, in her arms with her fingers on his neck, he felt he had jumped from the frying pan straight into the fire. The flames of want consumed him and his leg hurt like the devil.

God, he never wanted a repeat of what had happened between himself and Verity and his leg was swelling and aching more than it had done in the three years since the accident. It would be foolish to think that a beautiful young woman like Charlotte Fairclough would imagine herself wanting to be stuck with him. What was it that she had said of Nigel Payne?

'I value my freedom, Mr King.'

And she should.

The freedom to be whoever she wanted to be, to travel the world, to walk from one side of London to the other. She did not seem to him in any way to be static.

Static. The word held a dread that he could barely explain, but each year he was less mobile, more hampered, the pain greater, the leg worse. Soon he knew he would have to bring out the walking stick from the back of his wardrobe permanently and after that...

He shook his head.

'I think you value yours as well, Mr King.' Her words came through the fog.

'Pardon?'

'Your freedom. You seem to me like a man who uses up life wisely.'

Jasper nodded because it was the only reply he could give and as the music wound down into the final throes of the dance he felt as if he had missed a chance he might never get back.

Chapter Seven

Shepherding Charlotte back to his sister, Jasper was pleased that Verity and her friend were no longer present.

'Mrs Alworthy has gone home with a headache. You made a lucky escape from a woman like that,' his sister said. 'Her unending neediness would be wearying in the extreme, I should imagine. But to get back to the matter of why we are here, Viscount Harcourt is now in deep conversation with that man.'

Jasper looked around at the Viscount who was only a few yards away and, edging backwards, he brought Charlotte and his sister with him.

Charlotte, taking the cue, began to speak to Meghan in a quiet tone while he merely feigned interest, his whole being focused on what was being said between Harcourt and the stranger.

After five minutes of nothing he had almost given up when the other changed the topic completely.

'I want another girl, George. One more like the pretty blonde I saw you with the other day. The one with the fascinating birthmark on her chin.'

'My latest sweetheart is indeed beautiful and compliant, but I have already become tired of her.'

'So she's gone?'

'This morning. There's a replacement on the way as we speak. One with the same colouring, but with a more gentrified background. Working in a laundry hardly stimulates illuminating conversation.'

Both men laughed.

'Though she did have some experience in bed and was sweetly grateful for any titbit of kindness.'

The conversation ended there and Jasper turned to watch the two men separate and move away.

God. Charlotte would be aghast at Harriet's acquiescence.

A replacement? What the hell did that mean for Harriet White? Before he could think about it further the music heralded the arrival of a troupe of acrobats and the crowd leaned in to watch, Meghan among them.

Charlotte, however, had stayed back, her eyes alight with questions and, taking her hand in his, he led her to a small alcove at the very edge of the room, shaded by a line of bushy and ornamental trees.

Here there was some allowance of privacy, the candles alight on an old barrel alluding to a rustic atmosphere, but also adding to the concealment.

'Harriet was with Harcourt.' His words were measured.

'Was?' Her eyes darkened.

'She has been sent away somewhere.'

'By her own accord? Did she go because she wanted to?'

Jasper could not lie. 'More his wish, I think, though it does not sound as if she was coerced to come to him.'

'He got bored with her?'

Charlotte had read all that he was not saying well and she looked truly heartbroken.

'It does not mean she has been hurt. Harcourt is expecting a replacement which makes me think there is someone shifting women around. They would be a valuable commodity.'

'Unless they made trouble?'

'Was Miss White a woman who would be likely to do that? Make trouble?'

She shook her head. 'She was not.'

'Then we will find her, Miss Fairclough. We will find her and we will help any others who are also involved and no longer wish to be.'

Lottie felt the relief as a physical slam in her stomach and then as a thickness in her throat as she fought to keep back the tears.

He would help her. Jasper would help her even though he now suspected Harriet had been compliant in the whole sordid affair. She could not believe that he would. She could not believe that he might credit Harriet with a second chance and put his own life on hold and at risk to save a girl who had, unfortunately, been foolish.

'It would mean going back to the dangers of Old Pye Street?'

'I am sure I could handle that.'

'I want to come with you.'

'I know.'

Another slam of wonder struck her. He was not disputing her offer. He was not turning her away. He was trusting her to know her own mind and to support her in the doing of it.

She rose on her tiptoes and simply kissed him.

In gratitude and relief and in bewilderment and admiration.

And he kissed her back, with a hard want that singed her insides and took the sense from her head. Pressing in, she felt her world shift, from before to after, from then to now, and she knew that every point in her life going forward would be referenced from this moment, from this feeling.

He was not gentle or half-hearted. His mouth seared across her own, asking her to open to him and his tongue came in to taste as he pulled her around, one hand on her cheek and the other in her hair. Vigorous, potent and strong.

The clapping and shouting brought them back, the acrobats in a vertical line on each other's shoulders from the floor to the ceiling, the bright silk of their clothing flashing with colour.

A carousel, a merry-go-round, the successive flurry of sequence and activity counterbalanced against the stillness in their alcove. He was breathing heavily and so was she, caught in the moment, struggling for logic.

Jasper regained sense before she did, pulling away and straightening his neck tie. Tonight he wore a plain gold band on his forefinger with a single diamond which glinted in the light.

There were no words for what they had done.

It was a mistake.

I am sorry.

Can we find a more private place and do it all again?

She almost smiled at her last thought but didn't, the graveness of the longing they had exposed so very momentous. How did one retreat from this? Or go on?

For Harriet's sake she needed him to help her, but already in his eyes she could discern a distance, the more familiar reserve reasserting itself, detachment following close on its heels.

He is disappointed. In me.

She knew the truth of such a realisation and stepped back. This help he offered was simply out of duty to an old friend's sister and although the male in him had risen to the kiss she'd planted upon him she could tell he wanted nothing more to follow.

'We will find Harriet, I know it.' Her words were given impersonally as sense reached out with wisdom. 'And let us hope soon.'

Lord, he could barely believe what had just happened and in the middle of a crowded ballroom behind the very straggliest of ornamental trees. If the acrobats had not been performing their tricks, what scandal could have resulted? He doubted the return of sanity would have been so easy without the blaze of applause. He doubted he could have stopped, too, his frenzy peaking in a rush as she'd opened her mouth and welcomed him in.

He swiped his face with the sleeve of his jacket and turned away, from those lips and those eyes and the truth of dread he saw on her beautiful face. If his own heartbeat thundered like a runaway train, then Miss Charlotte Fairclough looked nothing but composed, her mind back again on the more important rescue of Miss Harriet White.

She walked in front of him into the crowd, her head tilted to watch the last antics of the performers now entangled in some impossibly difficult contortion. When the play had finished and a woman dipped into her bucket and threw red flowers into the crowd Charlotte caught one, holding it before her in quiet admiration.

Impossibly beautiful. Undeniably original.

He cursed these thoughts and looked away.

Not again. Not ever again for him, for Charlotte Fairclough deserved so very much more. He needed to find Miss White and he needed to find her fast and then he would depart for the north. He had a job that would take him away from London for a number of months and at this moment that looked to be a good thing.

He saw Nigel Payne making his way over to him and smiled, feeling the muscles in his jaw grate together as he did so. Sometimes late at night when his leg ached unbearably he cursed the man's stupidity for placing himself in such a dangerous position, right beneath the carriage as they were trying to fashion a coupling pin.

'You look to be enjoying yourself, Jasper?'

His body tensed. Had Nigel seen him kiss Charlotte Fairclough?

'The dance,' the other continued as a way of explaining. 'I am glad to see your leg so much better.'

Relief surged over irritation. Charlotte had walked over to talk with his sister so that he had a moment alone. Perhaps this was a good opportunity to learn a little more of the Viscount.

'Harcourt seems to me like a man who enjoys women?'

Payne smiled. 'Indeed, he does. He has a different escort every week and this week's catch, Caroline, was rather fetching with the mark at her chin. But I did hear that she had been sent back.'

'Back?'

'To wherever he procures them from. The girl was young. Too young, I thought, but then without the buffer of a good family and wealth her choices must be limited.'

Jasper decided to be honest.

'Caroline's real name is Harriet White and we think she was taken from Horseferry Road and a good job that the Fairclough Foundation had obtained for her.'

Comprehension filled Nigel's eyes. 'Which explains why you are here with Miss Fairclough. I wondered at your interest in attending this ball as you have not graced many of these social occasions in years. The thing is, I can't see Harcourt being unlawful, though if Lord Milner were involved in the transaction that would be entirely possible for I have met him a few times and I have never liked him. If I hear anything more though, I will send you word.'

'Who is Lord Milner?'

'A man Harcourt sees often. A man who Eloise and her mother have no time for when he comes calling. A man who does not care much for the laws and niceties of society. I should not like to cross him for I think he could be dangerous.'

And in that second Jasper remembered why he had leapt to Nigel's rescue all those years before. He was a good man and he meant well.

Tonight had been a fruitful one with the collection of clues. He had a place to start looking and the name of a man he had not considered before. He also knew that Harriet White now went under the new name of Caroline which must aid them in their search for her.

Their search. He frowned. He still had the problem of Miss Charlotte Fairclough and her presence at his side after the kiss was difficult, but he was thirty-three and long past the age of such vacuous drama. Swallowing his pride, he went to join her and his sister to one side of the room.

Lottie felt him there before she saw him, a shiver running down her spine as she turned. She needed to say something to him, about the kiss, about her sister, about anything that would make his withdrawal from her less personal. But he spoke before she did.

'Nigel Payne said that Harriet was here with Harcourt, though she goes under the name of Caroline now.'

He was all business and for that she was grateful.

'Was she happy? Did she say she was hurt in any way?'

'All I know is that she has been sent back. I also have the name of a man who might be involved in all this and a direction. If she was taken from the laundry, then perhaps it is to there that she will be returned and if not we can hope it will be to somewhere close by. Let us hope she has the sense to run.'

Meghan was now speaking to another woman she seemed to know so Lottie used this time left to her wisely.

'I realise that my kiss made you feel uncomfortable, Mr King, and of course I should not have ever done such a foolish thing because I hope that you will meet my sister Amelia at some point again and feel what you once did for her and she for you. Such a connection you both once enjoyed is valuable and unusual and wonderful and if you would only think about it I am sure that—'

He stopped her tumbling flustered words simply by holding up one hand.

'Despite what you think, Miss Fairclough, I have no feelings like the ones you speak of whatsoever for your sister and I never did. I also certainly do not plan to marry anyone any time soon.'

He could not have put his indifference more plainly and the awful realisation that she had betrayed both Millie and herself in her ill-thought-out words and actions dawned upon her.

It was a disaster. Mr King's honesty, Harriet's complicity and her own stupidity in imagining things could be so completely and utterly different.

Her clothes hung on her, marking her as the impostor she was, and those all around her felt foreign. This was not her place and these were not her people.

Amelia might not need to make any marriage whatsoever if her brother's plans of a fortune were realised and she wondered why on earth she had said anything to Jasper King at all.

She knew the answer, of course. She had tried to deflect the absurdity of her own interest in him given his hurtful indifference, a pitiful fact that was both nonsensical and selfish of her. Well, at least now she had a definitive answer about exactly where he stood on the subject of marriage.

He was not interested. In her or her sister.

The glory of being here dimmed completely and she was glad when Jasper excused himself from their company and went off to talk with some friends.

Three hours later, after one of the longest nights in her life, she was back at home and Claire, her maid who had been brought back earlier, was full of questions and curiosity.

'Did you have a wonderful time? You looked so

beautiful, Miss Lottie, and I imagine Mr King must have been impressed when he saw you so changed.'

'He was, but my cough has worsened after all the exertion and now I just want to lie down and be in bed.'

She coughed as if to underline her point and Claire fussed about her, finding camphor and a lemon drink and another warmer blanket for her bed.

When her maid finally left Lottie pushed back the covers and stood, glad to be by herself, glad for the silence and the darkness and the many hours until the morrow.

She would have to see Mr King again, of course, because she could not simply abandon Harriet, but...

One finger ran across the upper line of her lip in the way his had as the kiss ended, the tingling wonder of it echoing softly. She was twenty-two and this had been her very first kiss. Clandestine, scandalous and surprising in the way that it had stirred up her emotions so that desire snaked through her and settled in her stomach and lower.

This is what the stories spoke of and what her mother and father must once have known. This is what she had dreamed of even before she had perceived the power that it held, the intensity, the authority, the fire.

Her hand ran across her stomach, the answering tremors of knowledge there as well, and then they fell lower.

'Jasper.'

His name spilled out into the empty silence.

* * *

He walked the dark corridors of his town house, trying to iron out the ache in his leg. The dance had worsened the pain with the intricate steps and he felt exhausted. And sad.

The night had started well and finished badly. By the time they had all piled into the carriage to make their way home all he knew was a distance, the kiss from the early evening like an illusion.

Why the hell would Charlotte Fairclough have kissed him like that if she was only interested in finding a husband for her sister?

Nothing made sense, but then with her it very rarely had. He could tell Meghan had suspected something had changed between them, but did not want to ask, and for that he was grateful. He'd arrived home irritated, exasperated and vexed.

Women flummoxed him. He liked them for small, short spaces of time, but then they always wanted more. Or less in Charlotte's case. He dreaded meeting her tomorrow. God, he had known Miss Fairclough for only a matter of days and already she was taking over his thoughts.

His thigh gave way and he grabbed at the wall, holding himself up until the cramps passed. If his leg was no better by the morning, would he even be able to venture into the Irish Rookery and be of any use, a damaged adversary grasping on to what was left of his health by the skin of his teeth?

If Harcourt was foolish, then this Lord Milner sounded much worse and that was not giving any thought to the sycophants and hangers-on who would likely surround a man inveigled in a criminal underworld.

Once he might have dealt with all of this easily and that was the rub. He looked out of the window into the darkness of the night, the rain falling again and a similar dreary forecast for tomorrow. He hoped that they might ask Wilkes at the laundry some further questions and that Harriet White might have turned up again all by herself, realising the danger and foolhardiness of her actions.

The letter from Silas Fairclough was also a puzzle. He wondered why her brother had not written to his family for months in order to make sure that the three women were safe and well catered for. He could not believe Silas would have just left them in such a way.

When he slipped again he made his way to his bedchamber, dismissing his valet and reaching into the wardrobe for his old and familiar stick. The dimpled silver handle fitted into his hand like a glove, the mahogany of the wood still well polished. He would use this at home in his own company, but nowhere outside the walls of his house. He remembered the sound of it on the wooden floor from before, each click stabbing into his self-worth.

You have become a tortured cripple by your injury. I cannot be married to you because of this. I am sorry, Jasper. It would just be too hard and I am still so very young.

Verity's letter had been sent in the middle of his self-induced pity. Perhaps on reflection she had been sensible to distance herself, given he was well into the laudanum and probably not easy company any more to boot.

Still, the words hurt, try as he might to not let them. His first love. A woman he imagined he might spend his life with and be the one to bear his children. There was some intrinsic failure in such a break-down, some systemic collapse that had been hard to recover from.

He no longer loved Verity, he knew that. In fact, he doubted if he even liked her, but to see her to-night looking desperate and needy punched him in the stomach with the disappointment of it all. And then to be thrown off into the arms of her sister by Charlotte just moments after she had kissed him had sealed his fury.

He pulled a book from the small shelf at the side of his bed and sat down.

Travels to Discover the Source of the Nile by James Bruce.

Charlotte had said she read adventure stories about far-off places, too.

He shook her image away.

She had smelt of softness and lavender and some undetermined sweetness that he had breathed in with alacrity.

'God.'

It was the kiss. It stuck to him like the glue of some desperate need. It hounded his senses and brought him back to the moment when she had opened her mouth and simply let him in, all innocence and purity. He couldn't remember ever kissing anyone like that before, with such a craving that both surroundings and sense had simply evaporated.

'Please God, help me,' he said, but then could not quite work out what it was that he implored.

Peace. Sanity. Independence. A mix of grace and faith as well. To find Harriet White. To leave Charlotte Fairclough with no notion of these thoughts he was besieged with. To appear honourable and useful and strong.

He smiled. Mostly that. The walking stick hacked pieces of his certainty away and he wanted it back. He wished he could have started again with Miss Charlotte Fairclough and done everything differently.

But that wasn't quite being honest with himself because then she might not have kissed him and, truly, if all else came to nothing then at least he had that to remember her by.

Sitting against the pillows heaped at his back, he settled himself and opened his book. To be the first European to discover the source of the Blue Nile sounded impossibly exotic and for a Scottish man to travel in North Africa and Ethiopia all those years before without any map or direction was a wonder.

He deliberated on the thought of Charlotte reading this account of bravery and wondered at her own reading history. Silas Fairclough had always struggled with the thought of tying himself down and had been an adventurer at heart and so perhaps it was a family trait, this constant search for something else.

The quiet all around him descended as the clock in the corner of the room chimed out the hour of four. In the book James Bruce was finally on his way, sailing in a small vessel under a fair wind from Port Mahon around the cape of Ras el Hamra and landing at Bona, a considerable town two miles distant from the ancient ruins of Hippo Regius.

Shutting his eyes, he breathed in the image of the words. Foreign. Different. As far from his life here as he could possibly imagine.

His father's sickness and neediness had kept him in Liverpool for years and then the injury to his leg had sealed his fate. He was thirty-three and the books of adventures he read were a sad reminder of all that his life had not been. He had never travelled away from England once despite all the best intentions of doing so.

As he rubbed at his aching thigh he knew he could not now chance a journey to such far-off and exotic places. No, he was stuck here in his own bad health just as certainly as his father had been.

Pouring himself a brandy, he drank down the lot.

Chapter Eight

The banging at the door made her start and she looked at the clock in the kitchen.

Eight thirty.

Rosa O'Brian rushed through a moment later, her face full of wonder.

'I seen her, Miss Lottie. Harriet. I seen her with me own eyes, bundled from a carriage at the top of Old Pye Street. Just half an hour ago, it were, and although she looked straight at me she gave no sign of recognition.'

Such information had Lottie standing and calling for her coat and hat. 'We will find a hackney and go there immediately. I have a contact in the One Tun pub, a Mr Twigg, and we shall take Frank Wilkes from the laundry with us as extra security.'

But Rosa was having none of it.

'You can't just barge into men's business like that, Miss Lottie, else you will get hurt. We need the gentleman who helped us the other day. Mr King. He is the one who needs to deal with this.'

Lottie saw that Rosa was frightened stiff about being involved and so she did the only thing left to her.

'You stay here, then, just in case Harriet turns up at the Foundation. I will find Mr King and we will look for her.'

'And he will come?'

'I am certain he will. Now don't worry, it will all be fine and we will bring Harriet home.'

Claire, who had obviously been listening at the door, brought out her warm coat and hat. 'There's a hackney outside, Miss Lottie, for I just hailed him down. I am glad to hear you will get Mr King's help as it is only proper.'

Buttoning up her coat, Lottie nodded and jammed the hat on her head, grabbing her bag as she left. Outside it took her only a second to give the driver directions and then they were off.

Five moments later she stopped at the laundry on Horseferry Road, asking Wilkes to accompany her into the Rookery, for she knew it was not a place where a woman walked alone. Still, Frank Wilkes was quite slight and she missed the virile strength of Jasper, but given the circumstances between them there was no way she could ask him for help. She prayed to God that there wouldn't be trouble and that she would be able to find Harriet without any huge kerfuffle.

'This is a poor idea, Miss Lottie, getting involved in the affairs of others you know nothing about.'

Without answering Frank Wilkes, she pushed on across Grey Coat Street and the top of Horseferry

Road until they were in Old Pye Street. The weather had worsened, the rain falling heavily, and the place was largely deserted, there being no sign of either Harriet or of the carriage.

Half an hour. Forty minutes at the most. Harriet had to be here somewhere and standing still was not going to help find her.

Seeing movement in a window to their right, Lottie marched over and knocked on the door. A moment later it was wrenched open by a very old woman in a ragged nightgown, the shadows of others behind her.

'What do you want?' She appeared to be most put out by their visit.

'I am Miss Charlotte Fairclough from the Fairclough Foundation on Howick Place and we are looking for one of our girls who has disappeared. A Miss Harriet White who is now named Caroline, we think. She has blonde hair and brown eyes and a small birthmark just here.' Her finger came up to her own chin as she spoke.

'That's a description of half the young girls around these parts, Miss Fairclough. Primped and coloured for the men who never appreciate them. God knows I should be the one to tell them that, but they won't listen, these young ones. They go ahead and do what they think they must and get into trouble just like that.' She clicked old gnarled fingers and shook her head. 'If your friend don't want to be found, you'll never get her back, mark my words.'

Such a bleak statement had Lottie's spirits sink-ing, but she thanked the woman and they moved on to the next door and then the next one.

Half an hour later Lottie was almost beginning to despair when three men came from nowhere to confront them.

'Seems you are in the wrong place, Miss Fairclough, and poking your nose into things you should not. Wiser to turn around and leave the goings on in Old Pye Street to those who live and work here.'

These men were far more dangerous than the little group of youths who had confronted her the other day.

'I am not here to cause any trouble, but our Foundation has lost one of its girls and I have come to recover her. I do not want a fuss, but I do want her back.'

'Your interference in the fate of girls who ply their trade here is not welcomed. Besides, once they get to this place you have lost them already and no amount of cajoling will get them back.'

Wilkes at her side began to step away, but Lottie stood firm.

'Can you give her a message for me?'

'No.'

'Then you leave me with no choice but to involve the law.'

The biggest man planted himself in front of her and slapped her cheek before pushing her hard. Falling to the ground, she hit her head and her bonnet was lost, rolling in the breeze down the dirty cobbled street through heavy sheets of rain.

Frank Wilkes had run, gone even as she looked to

find him, and she was alone. With care she rose, her teeth chattering in shock, her face smarting with the ache of his violence.

'So Harriet is here? You have seen her?' The words came fierce and furious, all care gone now as she confronted him, this big dark-haired bully with two teeth missing at the front of his mouth and stinking breath.

'Get out of here.'

As he raised his hand again she could do nothing but wait for the force of it to hit her, praying to God that the end might be quick, that her mama and Amelia would not be too sad, that her brother would come home from the Americas for them and that Mr King might look back at their one beautiful kiss and wish with all his heart that there had been time for more. Shutting her eyes, she simply waited.

'Noooo!' The sound roared out from a few yards away and Jasper King was suddenly there, catapulting himself into the big man and sending both of them flying down on to the roadway. What he lacked in brawn he made up for in style, his fists pummelling the other in a way that bespoke of much training and expertise. Within a moment the bigger man lay still and Jasper stood, blood on his face, a scratch down the side of his cheek and his jacket ripped.

'Who wants to be next?' he snarled those words.

The miscreants stepped back and ran just as Wilkes had, as fast as they could go, turning the corner at the bottom of the road with speed and disappearing. The bully had roused and gone, too, though not quite at the same speed as the others. Lottie let out the breath she did not realise she'd been holding.

'How…did you find me?'

He didn't answer, merely grabbing her arm and pulling her with him, through the rain and the wind and the cold dank alley until his carriage was in sight.

'Get in. I need to see you safe.'

She did as he bade because her bottom hurt from where she had fallen, her cheek ached and her right wrist had been wrenched.

He shut the door behind them after giving his man an order to drive and then he faced her, his big frame filling the seat on the other side.

'Why the hell were you there alone? What crazy, foolish, stupid and irrational part of your brain thought that venturing into Old Pye Street by yourself and unarmed would have made sense?'

'I w…wasn't alone.' She had started coughing again and he waited until she finished, his eyes darker than she had ever seen them, the blood from his nose mixing with rain water and staining the white of his linen shirt.

'Then who the hell were you with?'

'Mr Wilkes.'

'A small unfit man who should have no part in such a stupid venture. Did he run? Did he damned well leave you alone with those three men in that street? Did he? Hell.' His fist lashed out and he punched the wooden frame of the carriage. Hard. Hard enough to splinter the first layer of wood.

She did not know what to say, his words and actions so frightening. Papa had always been measured and gentle, a man who rarely raised his voice, a man with a placid and calm manner.

Jasper, on the other hand, looked furious, his dark hair falling across his brow in wet curls and his knuckles bleeding from the punches that had connected first with the big man's face and now with the wooden structure of his conveyance.

One nail had been torn, she saw. All because of her.

'You are just damned lucky you are not dead, Miss Fairclough, lucky that they did not simply hit you over the head and throw your body in the river because they could have so very easily.' He stopped and took in a shaky breath, his eyes perusing the bruise that she knew must be showing on her cheek. 'I should have killed the bastard.' She could see the roaring fire of revenge unquenched in his eyes and knew suddenly the wonder of what he had done.

'I am sorry.'

He stopped at that and looked at her directly.

'Sorry? But that's not enough, is it, because you will do this again and again. Hell, and you can't even see it. You are five foot two at most and a woman. Insubstantial. Unpractised at violence. Weak.'

The regret she had been feeling turned into something less conciliatory at his words.

'Unpractised? Hardly. I see violence every day here in the Irish Rookery, every day against women just like me who cannot fight back and if I choose to try to do something to stop it then that is my business, Mr King, and you have no right to tell me how to handle it, no matter how insubstantial and weak you think I am.'

'No right. No right?' He seized her arm and hauled her over to his side of the carriage, a single easy movement completed before she had even the chance to protest.

'Why would your mother and brother leave you to your own devices? Why the hell is there no one here left to curb your foolhardiness? To make certain that you are safe? And why in God's name did you not send word to me about Rosa O'Brian seeing Harriet White earlier this morning?'

'I didn't think you wanted to be involved any more. With me.'

'Because of the kiss? Because my body was foolish enough to take your offer and turn it into something more. Something you didn't want? Something we both didn't want? God, help me.'

She burst into tears, suddenly and completely, and the crying brought back the coughing and before long she could barely take a breath, her eyes streaming and her nose running.

He held out another of his well-pressed perfect handkerchiefs and she took it. Gratefully.

'I never cry.' She said this after a moment or two and saw the slight upturn of his lips. 'Except with you,' she qualified and blew her nose.

At that he extracted a silver hip flask from his pocket and handed it over.

'Have a sip. It will help your chest at least.'

She did and nearly spat it out, so strong was the liquid.

'Whisky,' he explained, 'uncut and the very best. It will start to work in a moment. Drink again.' Tipping the flask with his hand, he made sure she did and this time the taste was less offensive. Almost welcomed. It had taken the shaking away and her cough did seem better. After a third sip he removed the flask from her hands.

'A drunkard is as bad as a fool and you won't be thanking me in the morning if you wake up with a sore head.'

The world had begun to soften around her, the hard edges lessened, the feeling of worry in her stomach further away. She had not found Harriet, but she had tried and she was glad that she had.

Jasper beside her was warm and safe even if his emotions ran high and he liked to be in control of every single situation. Without him today she could have been lying on a stone slab in the morgue ready to be buried right at the start of the Christmas season.

Her guardian angel. Dissolute and dishevelled, but here none the less, scolding her yet helping her and coming despite the distance that she had felt yesterday between them.

A tiredness overcame her, a weariness that she had felt for a long time now, ever since her brother had left, the Foundation taking every scrap of her energy and more. It was an unfair world and a harsh one, but here inside the luxury of the King carriage, all leather and mahogany, she was safe.

'Where are we going?'

'Nowhere. I asked the driver to simply drive until I tell him to stop.'

'I don't want it to stop. Not yet.'

He took her hand and held it, the warmth comforting.

'That's the whisky talking, Miss Fairclough.'

She giggled because perhaps it was and perhaps she was foolish to even think he wanted to spend some time in her company. But she did think it.

'When I saw you through the banisters that first time after you came calling on Amelia at the Foundation I thought you were Prince Charming, from the fairy tale. Your eyes were lighter,' she added, 'but they were always beautiful. Even now when you are angry they are so very beautiful.'

He frowned and banged on the roof and the carriage stopped, a footman coming to the door.

'Take us to the Foundation. Miss Fairclough needs to go home to sleep this off.'

'I'd rather stay here.' Her words were small as if she could barely say them. 'With you.'

Jasper had always thought the Fairclough Foundation was an austere one, but today in the wind and rain and with Christmas just around the corner it looked even more grim than normal.

Helping Charlotte inside, he was met by an ancient servant at the door and the same maid who had served him tea a few days back. She looked shocked.

'My goodness, Miss Lottie, what on earth has happened?'

In the light from the lamps the bruise on Charlotte's cheek was swelling and it was plain to anyone who looked that there had been a problem.

'We were set on in Old Pye Street.'

The woman shook her head. 'I told her not to go there, Mr King. I warned her of it right from the start and now...' She stopped and sniffed. 'Has she been drinking?'

'I gave her some sips of whisky to calm her down. It seems she took too much.'

'Then it's to bed for you, Miss Lottie.'

At that moment Charlotte simply fell against him, her balance unsteady, and without a word he picked her up.

'Where is her bedroom?'

'Upstairs, but you cannot possibly—'

He didn't let her finish.

'Where?'

The woman muttered under her breath and Jasper was sure he heard the words 'high and mighty', but let it go, following the maid and placing Charlotte down on a bed with a light blue coverlet. She looked so damn young and hurt lying there that he found himself gritting his teeth in an effort not to touch her and make sure she was quite all right.

As he reached the entrance hall again a man came out of a room to one side. He was of average height and good looking, but it was his mismatched eyes that drew attention. One was blue and the other was brown.

'Is there a problem here?'

He had a pleasant voice and a friendly smile and looked to be the only man at the Foundation Jasper had seen so far who was not well past fifty.

'I am Mr Jerome Edwards, the General Manager at the Fairclough Foundation.'

Jasper put out his hand and the man shook it. 'I'm Jasper King and I used to know Mr Septimus Clarke when he was here.'

'Ah. Mr Clarke retired about a year ago now and is living a more gentle life in the country with his sister. Did I hear there had been an attack?'

'You did. Miss Fairclough and I had gone to find news of Harriet Smith in the Rookery and ran into trouble.'

'I had heard the girl had gone missing. Do you have any idea as to who may have taken her, Mr King?'

'Not yet,' Jasper returned, 'but I am working on it.'

'If there is anything the Foundation can help you with, we would be most willing to try.'

When Jasper was once again back in his carriage and on his way home to Piccadilly he chastised himself for not asking Edwards if he might place some money in to the Foundation coffers to tide the Fairclough women over until Silas returned. He vowed he would visit the Foundation again in the next few days and offer such assistance.

Lottie woke hours later in the late afternoon, the winter sun finally appearing and slanting into her room. She had a searing headache she couldn't believe and, reaching for a jug of water on the bedside table, she took a long drink from the glass beside it.

She'd been undressed and put into her nightgown and her hair was dry. She could remember nothing save Jasper's anger when he had found her and saved her, but under that memory there was another softer one, sifting through a cloud. He'd brought her home, she was sure of it, after he'd offered her his hip flask with a liquid inside that had been the strongest she had ever tasted.

Lord. She had got drunk! The horror of it had her sitting up as she frantically searched for recall, finding nothing there save a vague impression of her foot hitting a painting on the wall as someone had carried her up the stairs.

She breathed out heavily with worry and a handkerchief on the table caught her eye. A different offering, for the other had been pressed and cleaned all ready to go back to him. This one held the stains of blood and wetness, the monogram of JS appearing through the ruin.

They had both been hurt, she knew that. She was perfectly sure of what had happened to her right up to a few moments after Jasper had offered her his hip flask. Then things became hazy.

When the door opened five minutes later and Claire appeared with a bowl of what looked like some thin soup, she groaned.

'You were drunk.' Her maid's words offered no embroidery. They also held much censure. 'Your mother would be straight back home if she were to know of this, and why should I not send word? Miss Lilian left you in my care and I cannot see any end to all this save for a disastrous one. The man is a devil to get you so drunk and both of you with blood on your face and hands and your clothes ripped. Lord help us, Miss Lottie, what am I to do with you save bundle you up and send you to Lady Malverly's Christmas party the moment you recover?'

'He saved me.'

That silenced her.

'Jasper King came to Old Pye Street and stopped them from hurting me.'

Claire sat down, her face pale. 'He wasn't with you? You did not go there with him? In the first place?'

'No.'

'Who was with you, then?'

'Frank Wilkes.'

Crossing her chest, Claire swore under her breath. 'That man is scared of everything.'

'He ran away. Mr King was furious to hear it.'

'As he should have been.'

'And then after he gave me some whisky to stop the coughing and the shaking. I think I took too much of it.'

'You most surely did. Far, far too much. My God, and I censured him for it. He left the house with the sharp edge of my words burning his ears when I should have been thanking the man.'

'What did he say when he arrived?'

'Very little. He carried you up to bed and told me to look after you.'

'And then he went?'

'But not before he left you this.' She took a book from her wide pocket and laid it down beside her.

Travels to Discover the Source of the Nile by James Bruce.

'He said to tell you he had read it and liked it.'

'I see.'

Lifting the tome, she felt the weight of it in her hands. She had told him once she enjoyed reading stories of far-away places and he had listened. The joy that was her normal state began to dribble back in.

He had also carried her up to bed. Her hands came to her mouth as she imagined that. Did he think her heavy? Had she said anything untoward to him? She vaguely remembered clutching on to a hard, broad chest and was mortified.

Jasper went straight home to change and then he visited Viscount Harcourt at his town house in St James's Square.

'Mr King?' There was question in the Viscount's voice as one of the servants showed him through into a library at the rear of the house. 'This is a surprise.'

'Thank you for seeing me.'

'You look a little worse for wear, if I may say so.'

Jasper decided to dive straight in to his reason for being here.

'I have been protecting Miss Fairclough from thugs in the Irish Rookery this morning. A young girl who holds the protection of the Fairclough Foundation has disappeared, you see, and we went to find her. The girl is the one you might know as Caroline.'

Harcourt paled quite considerably.

'Word has it that she was taken against her will in the first place and now she is nowhere to be found.'

Harcourt sat, pulling two glasses from a cabinet and a bottle of brandy down from a nearby shelf. Pouring generous amounts, he handed over a glass to Jasper.

'And you think I have had something to do with her disappearance?'

'I know you did.' His words were harsh, but he'd had enough. On his own admission, Harcourt, from his position of power, had been a party to using these women and it was time he felt the consequences.

For a moment the Viscount simply sat, but when he finally looked up Jasper knew that he had him.

'She was here, Mr King, you are right. For a few days she was my…consort and I treated her with respect. Well, with as much respect as the position implies, you understand. She was a willing lover. I did not hurt her and I certainly did not kidnap her either.'

'You sent her away?'

The other swallowed. 'I do not know how you know this, but it is true. She was not quite to my taste, after all, and there was another I held more interest in.'

'If I were to go to the constabulary with the details of the lost girl, it may not be easy for you. You may have been the last person to have seen her.'

'And will you?' Harcourt looked at him directly. 'Go to the constabulary, I mean?'

'Not if you help me with the pieces of the puzzle I cannot quite yet understand. Who is the man behind this supply of women?'

Jasper watched the man's fingers tap on the table for at least thirty seconds and then stop.

'Lord Milner has a friend who employs girls who want a good time. The friend's name is Mr Leonard Carvall and he can be found at this address.'

He quickly wrote out the man's direction and passed it over and Jasper saw that it was a house to the north of London.

'He is the man who supplies the girls. I pay— he supplies. I have nothing more to do with it than that. I swear it to be true on the grave of my sainted mother.'

'And the laundry in Horseferry Road? How is that involved?'

Harcourt looked genuinely puzzled. 'Caroline spoke of a laundry she worked in, but I have no idea if it is indeed the same one that you are querying about.'

'It is.'

'She said a man called Frank worked there if that is any help.'

'It isn't. Is the new girl here? The one you have asked for instead of Caroline.'

'She's not and I think I will limit my association with Milner in the light of these questions. My niece Eloise is constantly on at me to marry a good solid woman and settle and perhaps after this, I shall. I am becoming too old for such fright and I sincerely hope that this will be the end of it. I do not think I could weather a scandal if indeed something has happened to Caroline.'

Jasper drank the rest of his fine brandy and stood.

'If you see Carvall before I do, can you tell him that I am looking for him?'

'I won't see him, Mr King, for I have never met him personally.'

Tipping his head, Jasper left the Viscount refilling his glass and looking highly out of sorts.

Leonard Carvall's address was closed up and empty. A bogus direction, a place of shadows and mirrors, aiding a man who worked at brokering other people's ruin.

When Jasper asked a neighbour about the house he was led to believe the place had been unoccupied for at least three months.

The image of Charlotte in the rain with her wet hair and damaged cheek came to him, the thick meaty fist of the biggest thug about to rain down upon her fragile bones terrifying.

He blinked twice, hard, trying to disperse the memory, but it kept returning again and again.

What if he had been too late?

What if Twigg from the One Tun pub had not sent him word about Charlotte being there asking her inflammatory questions?

What if he had not instructed his driver to go faster and then faster again?

Charlotte Fairclough would have been dead. A

small crushed shape on the cobblestones of the Irish Rookery, all the life in her gone.

He remembered her words when she was drunk, soft improbable things that spoke of more than indifference. Drink muddled one's brain and he could hardly take such utterings as gospel. Still, the hope of it was there, in a warmth about his heart.

He needed to go home and rest his leg because the cramps were threatening, but he did not. Instead he went to the One Tun to see the publican.

Twigg was in the back room, a woman dressing the cut above one eye with an ointment that smelt strongly. The publican sent her away as soon as the doctoring was finished.

'They found out I sent you a note, Mr King,' he said as he looked up, 'and I'm lucky to escape with only this.'

The hand he used to gesture to his face was grazed, too, and digging into his pocket Jasper laid out two gold coins on to the table before him. 'This is in payment for your note warning me that Miss Fairclough was here asking questions. If I were you, I'd use it to employ a few of your own men here as security. Do you know a man named Leonard Carvall?'

'I've heard the name, all right.'

'I think he's behind all this and I need to find him.'

'He isn't from around the Rookery and, if you want my opinion of where things presently stand, I would say that those you seek are not pleased with your interest in them.'

'Or that of Miss Fairclough?'

Twigg shook his head. 'The Fairclough Foundation holds a strong pull in these parts and there would be hell to pay if they killed her.' He stopped. 'There'd be too many questions to answer, for even with all the criminal activity there is a loyalty here to those who try to help and the Fairclough family definitely does that. I think it was more of a scare-off tactic.'

The tight knot of fury inside Jasper loosened a little, though the fright they had given her was still deplorable.

'I will be asking around for any information, Mr King, for it's become personal now for me as well and if I hear anything you will be the first to know.'

Once Jasper was back in his carriage he wanted to return to the Foundation just to see how Charlotte fared, though he could not do that without inciting much question. Meghan had also asked him to dinner, but he was too tired to even think about eating and his torn-off nail hurt like hell.

He listed his injuries in his head and then went on to catalogue Charlotte's. Leonard Carvall and his cronies would pay for the injuries somehow and he was glad to have Twigg on his side.

He was also glad that the Fairclough Foundation held so much power in the Rookery, for it was a protection. He wished he could have whisked Charlotte away from the danger of the place and deposit her in Piccadilly where the genteel ties of manners held a safety.

This thought had him swearing again because he did not quite understand what it meant for them both.

Chapter Nine

Lottie had not seen Mr Jasper King at all yesterday and she'd been glad for it, holed up in her room with a headache and a body that hardly felt like her own.

She would never drink whisky again, she swore it on Nanny Beth's departed soul and on the memory of her father. She had stayed in bed most of the previous day reading the book that Mr King had sent her from cover to cover and rejoicing with James Bruce when, after battling malaria, he made his triumphant final march. The source of the Blue Nile of the Ancients was in a little swamp with a hillock rising from its centre and the explorer had picked up a coconut shell and filled it with water before making a toast to King George the Third as well as to Catherine, Empress of all the Russians.

Even feeling nauseous and sick, she could imagine him there with his guide and his small band of fellow travellers and the names of the places he had passed to reach the source were marvellous and exotic ones.

But today she was restless and wished that Jasper would call. Perhaps he was still disgusted with her for going alone into Old Pye Street or for her drunkenness in his carriage.

She'd liked to have sent him a note to thank him for his help and for the book and for carrying her up the stairs at the Foundation when she could not have walked herself.

But she didn't send one. She had just enough pride left.

Standing up, she walked to the window and looked out. It had finally stopped raining and for a change patches of blue sky could be seen among the scudding clouds. Christmas Eve was only just over a week away and she had not hung a single decoration anywhere.

She'd need to leave for the Malverly affair, too, before long. Mama had allowed her a fortnight to get better and that deadline was fast approaching. She frowned and drew her finger across the glass. If she left London, she'd never see Jasper again, she knew it, and she wouldn't find Harriet either.

The tightness in her chest had finally begun to abate and for the first time in days she was not subject to the fits of coughing she'd become accustomed to.

The letter came from Mr King just before lunch asking if she could accompany him to talk with a woman who had been in the employ of someone of interest. It would be a short safe trip to the north of London, according to the letter, and he would have her home by five o'clock in the afternoon.

Someone of interest? Lottie knew this message was to do with Harriet, but she could not quite work out who the woman might be.

'I hope there will be no problems,' Claire said after Lottie told her about the invitation. 'I am not certain any more about you being alone with Mr King…'

'Oh, we have been over this, Claire. Mama would be right behind any effort to help Harriet.'

'What of Mr King's sister? Can she not accompany you?'

'I am unsure. Perhaps she will be there. We will find out in an hour, but for now I should go and get dressed.'

She chose a light grey frock that she had always liked, her thick hair secured with pins at her nape. Her jacket was of a dark blue wool, pin-tucked on the sleeves, the collar high and frilled. On her head she wore the only bonnet she now owned.

Today she felt herself. Not the primped and perfect Miss Fairclough from the ball or the one who had modelled her sister's severe hairstyle. Today there was a lilt in her step and a smile in her heart, and the bruise on her cheek had faded into almost nothing.

When he did arrive right on time Jasper's face appeared a lot worse than it had done two days ago. The skin under his eye was reddish-black and the cut on his jaw was swollen. She didn't even glance at his hands.

'I am fine.' He said this as she opened her mouth to speak. 'My injuries look worse than they feel.'

'Harriet had better be grateful then, when we do

find her.' The stray dog had come in to the room at the sound of his voice and Lottie used the moment to further the hound's cause. 'He likes you. He never does this with anyone else.'

Jasper laughed and stepped back to allow her to proceed him through the door. Outside he helped her into his carriage and they both sat, the door closing behind them.

'I spent yesterday looking for a Mr Leonard Carvall, who seems to have a lot to do with the procuring of women, and I found a lady who knew of him and who was more than willing to talk. She told me if I came back she'd have another younger girl to give me information that ought to be known. When I enquired whether I could bring you along, your association with the Fairclough Foundation was received with great interest and she agreed.'

'My goodness. Do you think it could be Harriet?'

'I doubt it, but perhaps the younger woman has seen Harriet or knows of her.'

Lottie nodded. 'I cannot believe you would still want to include me in your plans after...' She stopped, finding it difficult to carry on.

'After your poorly judged solo outing?'

'It was foolish and if this was the result...' She gestured to his face and hands.

'Oh, I have had far worse than this, Miss Fairclough.'

This was drawled, lazily, an undertone in the words that made her blush. But she didn't falter.

'Your leg?'

For just a second shock blazed from his eyes before it was hidden.

'Mr Payne indicated to me at the party that it was
his fault somehow. I sensed your sister may have felt
the same.'

They were now heading north and it was lovely
to be sitting here far from anyone with just Jasper as
her company. The sun was out today again giving the
landscape a jaunty edge.

'Accidents happen, Miss Fairclough.'

'But you saved him. Mr Payne said that you did
and when I talked to Miss Proctor later in the night
she said you were a hero.'

'A hero? Now there's a word that comes in many
shades.'

'You do not think you were one?'

'Payne was helping me on a difficult job at a train
yard just outside Liverpool. I had invented a coupling
that saved a good few minutes of time for those wanting to unlink carriages. As we were fastening it into
place he didn't grasp the danger and hammered out
a pin he should not have.'

'Yet it was you who was hurt?'

'When the coupling broke I had just enough time
to push him to one side.'

'And you?'

'I landed where he had been and the carriage shell
came down across my thigh. Part of it was embed-
ded in my leg.'

Lottie imagined the pain and the shock.

'Did Mr Payne get you out?'

'He fainted. I got my own leg free and crawled to find help. Luckily others were about when it happened and they rushed me to a doctor.'

'Poor Mr Payne. You got the injury, but he got the guilt. Nanny Beth used to have a saying that every man is guilty of all the good he didn't do.'

'Miss Fairclough?'

'Yes, Mr King?'

'Most people never ask about my injury, yet you use quotes from Voltaire to try to mitigate my feelings.'

She smiled. 'At the Foundation we are taught the value of speaking about difficulties in the past. And on that note, I do blame you a little for the headache I endured yesterday. Your whisky was dangerously addictive, though the book you bequeathed me was wonderful.'

'You've read it already?'

'Right through.'

His eyebrows arched and he tipped his head. 'You are like your brother Silas. Did you know that?'

'I doubt it highly. Always my family have admonished me for being the odd one out.'

'He is an adventurer and yet you were the one who went alone into one of the most dangerous alleys in the Rookery to locate your friend. I'd say that was brave.'

'Or careless. Frank Wilkes was the wrong man to ask for help as I didn't comprehend how scared he'd become. You, on the other hand, are scared of no one, Mr King. Where was it you learned to box?'

'At a boxing academy in Regent Street, fists and fortitude being all the rage fifteen years ago. Engineering takes you into many different situations and Liverpool is not a city that is always safe.'

'I'd like to be so very competent.'

Charlotte Fairclough made him laugh and Jasper thought that it had been a long while since he had found anyone able to accomplish such a thing. She was honest, too, in her apology and in her compassion.

The bruise on her cheek had faded and if she had been cursed by a headache yesterday from his whisky there were no signs of that either. Today her hair was escaping its strictures again, the curls falling from their pins even as she sat there, her eyes wide with interest.

'I've seldom ventured into this part of London. It's like a different world. So leafy and tidy.'

'Mrs Selena Greene is the wife of a successful businessman.'

'And how did you find her?'

'She is the cousin of my valet. He heard me mention Leonard Carvall and said he had never liked the man. It seems Mrs Greene does not either.'

A few moments later they arrived at the home of the Greenes and were shepherded through to a small room on one side of the entranceway. Mrs Greene stood just inside.

She was a handsome woman of about forty, accompanied today by a younger version of herself, right down to the red hair they both sported.

'Mr King. Miss Fairclough. Let me introduce to you my niece, Miss Annette de la Fauvre. She works in a pub Mr Carvall often frequents.'

'I am very pleased to meet you both.' The French name of the girl sat oddly across her West Yorkshire accent as Lottie hurried in with her questions.

'My friend, Miss Harriet White, has gone missing from Horseferry Road in the Irish Rookery, but we think she goes by the name of Caroline now. Would you know of her?'

Annette looked thoughtful. 'There are a number of young women in the employ of Leonard Carvall. I hear them talk, you see, sometimes in the pub when they accompany him and it seems that they are treated almost as slaves.'

Lottie's face paled.

'They are not allowed outside and are shifted from place to place where the need arises. There is talk they may have been taken against their will and can never escape. Mr Carvall is a man who is both dangerous and ill tempered, so I should not like him to know I have been here speaking with you.'

'He will not, you have my word upon it.' Jasper made that promise and the two women relaxed somewhat.

'Where is the pub you speak of, Miss de la Fauvre?' He needed a place to begin, a location that could be checked out.

'In Vine Street. It is called the Marquis of Granby

and I am one of the barmaids. It is a well-paying job
for what it is I have to do, but lately—' She stopped.

'Tell them, Annette. Tell them what you have told
me.' Mrs Greene was insistent.

'Lately Mr Carvall has been watching me in particular and he has said things which have made me
feel uncomfortable. I also think he is drugging the
younger girls to make them docile and I think that
many are there against their will. My aunt has offered
to pay my passage to the Americas to get me out of
harm and I have accepted. I leave England next week.'

'Well, that is wonderful news and I wish you the
very best of luck.' Lottie said this and clasped the
girl's hand, eliciting a smile from Mrs Greene.

'A woman should have the rights to her own body
and no man should take that permission from her. If
you observe him, Mr King, you might also be able
to find the missing girl, though he surrounds himself with less-than-moral people so I would watch
your back.'

'You have been most helpful, Mrs Greene.'

'Tom, your valet, is my favourite cousin and he
was insistent we could trust you.'

'Which you most certainly can.'

Five moments later they were back in the carriage
and Charlotte looked furious. Well, it was better than
sorrow, Jasper thought, and bade the driver on.

If Mr Carvall had drugged Harriet, Lottie thought,
then it just made the finding of her all the more difficult. Drugs and alcohol and their effects were a big

part of the misery in the Rookery and it was seldom those who had been under their influence were ever removed from them.

'After the work at the Foundation I thought I might be immune to the evil things one person does to another, but I find, after all, I am not.'

'I shouldn't have brought you with me. It was a mistake.'

Jasper was going back to being controlling again and Lottie had had enough.

'I do know what happens between a man and a woman in the sale of flesh, Mr King. I understand those implications, but drugs are something else entirely. I am unsure if we would be able to extract Harriet from their persuasive grasp.'

'It's early days. If we can find her before a dependency settles—'

She broke across him. 'You cannot know what I have seen when people take them for any time. It is an indescribable horror and poor Harriet will be much changed because of it.'

He shook his head. 'Carvall will likely be using laudanum. At first it's almost a joy to feel nothing, it's only later the rot sets in.'

The truth surged through her.

'You are speaking about yourself? You know what it is like to be addicted to the laudanum?'

'I do.'

The words made her start and she did not quite know how to go on from here. The iniquitous opium dens came to mind, places of immorality and depravity. Had he been in those?

'Do you still use it?' Stiffening, she waited for his answer.

'No.'

A simple and small word encapsulating a thousand hours of agony. It took a soul far braver than any she'd ever known to wrench themselves free and live.

'It was for the pain in my leg, you understand. I went for months when I could not sleep and any oblivion was welcomed.'

Secrets. Hidden in sorrow.

'But I was able to pull myself free with the help of my sister. She came and rescued me when I had given up on hope. I offer my own poor history to you as a way of courage, Charlotte.'

The use of her name came unexpectedly, a small intimacy that made her draw in breath.

'Harriet White is young and fit, I presume. If we find her soon, she will recover, I give you my word upon it.'

'Thank you.'

She wanted to ask him more questions, about his leg, about his pain, about the hopelessness that might drive a man like him to depend on a drug and about Meghan's part in making certain he stayed safe. But he had been more than forthcoming today and she did not wish to ruin such directness by pushing things further.

He had given her a gift and his candour and frankness warmed her.

'My town house is only a few streets away. If you would like something to eat and drink, we could go there. It's more difficult in public to be alone.'

Alone.

A feeling of excitement shot through her, the kiss from the other day still very much on her mind.

Should she say yes? Would he kiss her again if she did so? Would there be staff there who might censure her or members of his family? Claire, her maid, would tell her to return home immediately if she were present, but suddenly Lottie didn't want to. She wanted to take a risk and live. She was twenty-two, after all, and this could be her very last chance of feeling free.

She had sent a message to her mother yesterday explaining that she was still recovering from her cough and would need another three or four days to make the journey without problems. She had phrased the letter in a way that would not make Lilian worry and return to London. She hoped it would suffice.

'Thank you. I would like that.'

A thrill of consequence shivered through her though when she looked up at Jasper he did not seem to be feeling the same. If anything, he looked more severe, more stern, the injuries to his face adding to the danger.

After a quick word to his driver they were on their way and it took only a few minutes before they were pulling up to the imposing façade of his town house in Piccadilly. It was much bigger than she might have imagined it to be, the road it sat on beautiful and quiet.

'Are your parents here?' She had to ask this, because if they were she would not go in.

'My father died almost three years ago and my mother when I was very young.'

'My papa died of typhus when I was a girl. There was an epidemic of it that raced through the Foundation and everyone was sick. Mama said it was a miracle that our family had survived it intact and then the very next week my father was gone. Quickly and without much of a goodbye, as if some celestial being had heard Mama use the words and wanted to smite our family for gloating.'

'Charlotte?'

'Yes?'

'You talk a lot when you are nervous. Did you know that?'

Swallowing, she shook her head.

'I would never hurt you. I promise it.'

And she believed him. Implicitly and absolutely.

She wished just then that she might have been able to put her glasses on to see his eyes in clear detail, but they were left at home on her bedside table because she had not wished to show him again her broken spectacles. Perhaps that was a vanity that she would be punished for. Perhaps she should be honest.

'We are not a wealthy family, Mr King. At the moment my mother and sister and I are hanging on to our existence by our fingernails and unless Silas returns some time soon after the New Year we will need to close the Foundation, for the rent is excessive and the money is dwindling.'

'Why are you telling me this?'

'Because you are wealthy and you have said your resources are many and my family holds none of the largesse that yours does. I cannot even afford to have my glasses fixed, so if this invitation to eat should allude to other things as well then it is far better to put an honest foot forward than be rebuffed for a false one and regret it later.'

'Other things?'

He had shepherded her in now past a man who had opened the door and into a side salon. He closed the door behind them.

Oh, my goodness, he looked so beautiful standing there, strong and damaged and magnificent. Was he playing with her? Surely it should have been her exquisite sister here before him, all auburn hair and glittering green eyes.

'I am not beautiful like my sister, Mr King, I know it, but still a woman like me has her dreams and hopes and if—'

He stepped forward and his mouth covered her own.

God, he wanted her. He wanted Charlotte Fairclough like he'd never desired any woman before, with a desperate burning need, and he knew it had been a huge mistake on his part to bring her here.

She would be a virgin and the expectations she had of a dalliance were nothing like the ones a more experienced woman might harbour.

But he couldn't stop his tongue seeking entrance

and one hand turning her head so that he could taste her deeper. Ambrosia. The softness of her curves moulded to his body, full breasts felt through the wool of her gown where the cloak she wore had fallen back, his fingers there cupping the flesh, flicking across a nipple standing proud under his ministrations, her curls all escaped now and descending in gold-brown waves down her back.

How could she think she was not beautiful? How could she not see that her beauty was so much more than the insipid version society had deemed to favour? She was like fire in his arms with those whisky eyes and pale skin and a mouth that was swollen and reddened.

He never lost control; discipline, limit and constraint always held firm in the face of what he had been through and yet here his self-professed restrictions were a weak nothing compared to Charlotte's sultry and honest sensuality.

He could not stop, his leg riding between her thighs, bringing her closer, edging into his hardness, feeling his way. The warmth of her centre was only the thickness of wool from him and she was clutching him closer in her want for more.

The knock on the door had him turning as he pushed her behind him, trying to find reality, the blood thundering in his ears like drums, every single fibre in his body burning in shock.

'Your sister Mrs Gibson has called by, Mr King. She is waiting to be seen in.'

'Thank you, Larkin.'

The door shut behind his departing butler.

'Hell.'

Her expression looked as flabbergasted as his probably did and he took in breath.

'I will have to see her.' He hardly knew what to say.

Charlotte was tidying her hair, her fingers then on the line of her gown, straightening the skirt. She looked small and brave and alarmed.

'It will be all right. I promise.'

'Will it?' Her answer came back quickly, thrown into the mix without thought, and then Meghan was there, her countenance sharp and perplexed both at the same time.

'Miss Fairclough? I did not expect you to be here.'

'We have just come from the house of a woman with a knowledge of where Miss Harriet White might be, Meg.'

'Business, then?'

Jasper did not like the smile that accompanied his sister's query and his eyes clashed with hers.

'Exactly.' He did not have her inclination for humour given his body ached with the incompletion of what Charlotte and he had started and which had been so abruptly stopped. 'Would you like a drink, Meghan?'

'Not today, for I have a meeting at the Women's Temperance League this afternoon. I just called in to say hello. Your face looks damaged, Brother.'

'The result of a run in with the self-styled protectors of the prostitution racket in Old Pye Street.'

'What do their faces look like?'

'Worse.'

'You are playing with fire, Jasper. Make sure you are not further burnt.' Her glance took in them both in a single knowing stare. 'Well, I have to go or I shall be late.'

Jasper laughed, almost certain that she would not be. Meghan always left hours between appointments so that she would not be tardy.

'Would you like me to drop you off somewhere on my way, Miss Fairclough?' His sister had changed tack now and he cursed her for doing so. A simple query infused with a great deal of meaning. But Lottie stood her ground.

'No, but thank you. There are a few things I still need to ask your brother about.'

'Well, good for you. My advice would be to make sure he is aware of your intentions.'

Then she was gone, the door closing behind her, only the perfume she used still in the air left behind. Wild roses and musk.

'Your sister knows.'

Lottie felt breathless and uncertain, the play between Jasper and Meghan unlike anything her family ever indulged in. Half-truths and innuendo. Warnings and a ribald humour. She could not understand it.

'She won't say anything.'

'You are sure?'

'I am. She wants me to be happy. She is constantly worrying about me.'

'And are you that? Happy?'

'Yes.'

A hard core of worry melted and she felt herself relax.

What was it between them that made sense fly right out of the door when he kissed her? Was this normal, this strange tear in time and place so that they both fell through to somewhere else entirely? She thought of Millie. Should she believe him when he said he was not interested in her sister? He had also said that he would not marry and that was another worry.

She did not want him to touch her again, not now, not here, not after an almost-discovery. She felt frightened by her reactions and panicked by their implications.

A few moments before she would have laid down with Jasper here on the floor in a room with an unlocked door and allowed him everything. Just like in the ballroom.

Unbelievable.

Incendiary.

Like a harlot.

If Mrs Gibson had not arrived when she had…

'I am sorry…' he began to apologise, but she held up her hand.

'It was not just your fault, Mr King.'

'Jasper. I think we are long past the other.'

'Jasper,' she repeated and felt an unhealthy need to laugh. Which she didn't, of course, the seriousness of their near-disaster still close. If Meghan had arrived ten minutes later, what could have happened, then? Would she now be the sort of girl who often came calling at the Foundation? Pregnant and alone, the realisation of her foolishness barely believable and the future in front of her dim.

Ladies of worth did not make love after one kiss with a man they hardly knew. They kept a suitor dangling for weeks or months and made him promise things that would not leave them high and dry. Sensible options. Alternatives that gave them purchase to bargain with, things like promises of marriage and for ever.

How often had Mama drilled this into both her and Amelia?

'Do not give your virginity away for free, girls. Make sure it means something and is treasured by the man you love.'

The man you love.

Did she love him? Jasper King? Could it happen this quickly with just a week's worth of being together?

Yes.

Her world spun with the possibility of it, but he hardly looked as if he might suddenly proclaim his undying devotion to her. No, he looked distracted, if anything, and wary, the kiss of a moment ago forgotten in the unexpected visit by his sister.

He was a man of the world, with a trail of lovers behind him. Meghan Gibson had told her that as they had prepared for the Harcourt ball. His next words confirmed his indifference.

'The Marquis of Granby tavern Miss de la Fauvre

mentioned is known to me. I shall go tonight and see if Mr Carvall is drinking there.'

'I could accompany you if it would help.'

'Absolutely not.'

Lottie wished she might have argued otherwise, but she knew that her lack of any skills in the art of self-defence would put them both at risk.

Still, she didn't quite give up.

'I could stay in the carriage with the driver and the footmen just to make sure you returned safely? I would not move from the conveyance, I promise it.' She held her hand above her heart.

He hesitated, which was hopeful.

'I have no one who I need to answer to at the Foundation, so there would be no objections if I was to come.'

'A fact that seems to worry me more than it does you.'

'It's just that I am expected at the Malverly Christmas party before too long and I do not want to miss the chance to be of assistance.'

'I see.'

A sense of stillness permeated everything, folding her into quiet. She felt the ache of sadness inside her because after that she would lose him. To his business. To life. To for ever.

Jasper knew that he should say something about the kiss, but he could not quite think what to say. Charlotte Fairclough was beautiful and brave and good, but she was not for him.

He would ruin her.

Better to let her go so that another younger, less-damaged man could steal her heart and make her happy. He would leave London straight after the Christmas festival and Charlotte was due to rejoin her sister and mother very soon.

He knew he should not agree to taking her tonight to the tavern, but with the days between them running down so quickly he found himself at odds with logic.

He wanted her to come. He wanted to see her again before the morrow, to know that she was safe and secure and protected. It would not be dangerous if she waited three streets away with his driver and two footmen. There could be no harm in it and he could tell her then immediately of any discoveries about Miss White that he made. If things went really well he might even be able to bring the girl back to Charlotte in the conveyance and then it would be finished. Over. He did not like the catch in his throat at the thought of never seeing her again, never kissing her and feeling her in his arms.

Had the knock on the head the other day made him foolish? He could see his sister thought that he was different, her expression today all censure and puzzlement. Another bridge to build. He would visit Meghan tomorrow and explain.

What, exactly?

I kissed Miss Fairclough until my world exploded and I could not fathom what might happen next.

He smiled because he imagined what his sister might say back to him, then.

'I will go on ahead of you and my driver will pick you up at seven. That way you will not need to wait so long. Wear something warm because the weather tonight is supposed to be colder than it is now.'

'I will.' She sounded breathless and young.

Only hours till he saw her again.

'And tell no one your plans, for a man like Carvall will have his spies in places that may be surprising.'

'You mean in the Foundation.'

'Perhaps. It seems the laundry is one of his haunts for business.'

'I can think of no one who would be so deviant. I'd trust every one of our employees with my life for most of them have been with us for years.'

'Then that is heartening.'

She could hear the ring of hollowness in his tone and thought he did not trust easily. Perhaps not even her?

'The dog at the Foundation is still searching for a home. I wondered if you had thought any more about giving him one?'

'I have not.' His reply was marked in a reluctance. 'And if I did procure a pet she would be small and well-mannered and a purebred.' There was definite humour in his voice now and she liked that there was.

'Well, it's always a good thing to be flexible, I find. Then life does not disappoint you.'

He began to laugh. 'Do you ever take no for an answer, Miss Charlotte Fairclough?'

'Don't make up your mind just yet. Promise me.'

She held out her hand and he took it in a hand-shake.

'I promise.'

Jasper and the wary stray both needed someone in their lives, for trust and companionship, and the mongrel reminded her of him in more ways than she could count. He was watchful and careful and stood apart from the world. Perhaps she would even bring the dog with her tonight.

Sensing her need to go, Jasper shook his head. 'You will not stay for lunch.'

'I think that under the circumstances I should leave.'

On his command a servant had come into the room and waited quietly at the door.

'See that Miss Fairclough is returned home to Howick Place, Wilson, and make sure to watch her passage until she is inside the gates.'

Protection. It never left him. She smiled and turned to depart.

Chapter Ten

The evening started badly from the very beginning.

The man Jasper presumed was Leonard Carvall was drinking in a large side room and he was imbibing heavily. He was also in the company of four men who did not look savoury.

Taking a seat by the door, Jasper watched the group for a moment and then beckoned the barmaid over. She was a lusty and well-endowed girl wearing her bodice low. Consequently, when she crouched over him, he nearly had a view of her navel and beyond.

'A whisky, please. The best you have and send one each to the group at that table.'

'Is there to be a message to go with it?'

Jasper considered. 'There is. Tell them that I would like a word with Mr Leonard Carvall and alone if I may.'

'He is otherwise engaged, sir.'

'Tell him.'

He did not soften the command and the woman scurried off.

Nonchalantly he brought a purse of gold from his pocket, throwing it on the table before him. Eyes were everywhere in a place like this and he leaned back, pleased when the bargirl returned with his whisky. It was seven thirty and Jasper knew his carriage with Charlotte Fairclough inside would easily be in place by now.

'Mr Carvall will be with you shortly.'

He opened the purse and extracted a coin, putting it in her hand and smiling.

'Thank you.'

Her fingers clenched around the treasure. 'You are more than welcome, sir, and if it's a good time you are after my name is Alice.'

He watched as she moved away. He'd sat here deliberately. No one could creep up on him and he had a full view of the door and the windows.

Sipping his whisky, he stretched out his legs. He knew Carvall would make his move soon and that it was only a matter of waiting. If he could offer him enough of an inducement to let Harriet go, it might well be possible to free her simply with words.

All thoughts of that plan were scratched, however, as another woman materialised from a place behind the bar and walked across to him. A young blonde woman with brown eyes and a birthmark on the side of her chin. But she did not look entirely happy, a bruise around her mouth slathered with thick make-up. Her dress was undone so that the small shape of her breasts showed under the petticoat beneath. He could tell she was scared because she kept looking over towards Carvall, the pulse at her throat a fast and solid beat.

'Can I be of assistance to you, sir?'

He decided to play along to see the lie of the land. 'In what capacity?'

'Any you desire,' she returned flatly and sat on the empty chair opposite. 'My name is Caroline.' Her bottom lip was cut and he wondered what she must be thinking of his own wounds.

Leaning in, he gestured her forward as though he hoped for a certain closeness or a better look, his hand winding her fingers into his own.

'I am a friend of Miss Fairclough, Harriet, and I am here to bring you home.'

This was said quietly in a whisper and, to give her her dues, she hardly reacted, her pupils widening and her breath hitching, but no larger distress that others might act upon.

'It cannot be possible, sir.'

'Smile,' he said and she did. He brought out another coin and placed it down between them.

'Where is your room?'

All humour disappeared. 'Upstairs, sir.'

Well trained. Impossibly nervous. Dispirited.

'When I give you another coin I want you to walk out the front door and keep going.' He bought her fingers to his mouth, kissing her knuckles, his tongue running across the lines of her wrist as if a proposition was what he was here for. 'Turn left and then take the second road on the right. Miss Fairclough is there waiting for you in my carriage. She will return you to the Foundation.'

Hope flared and her teeth worried her bottom lip. 'There are men here who…'

'Let me worry about them.'

He opened his purse and made much of depositing another golden coin in her palm. With a tremble she stood and turned for the stairs, changing direction at the very last moment and going straight out through the open door.

'Hey.' Carvall's group were finally moving, chairs thrown back in their haste to go after the escaping Miss White. 'Get her.'

The whole table erupted into movement which allowed Jasper the chance to grab a stool and stop the first man and then the second from following. He was at the door now, too, slamming it shut with his foot as another man with Carvall loomed down over him. The next was more difficult and had some training in the art of boxing. A meaty fist slammed into Jasper's thigh and then his mouth, the pain from the first winding him and bringing small black spots across his vision.

Carvall was gone. Instantly. But three others had taken his place and were advancing on Jasper.

No one had followed Harriet, though, and he knew that he'd given the girl enough of a head start to be able to reach his carriage without obstruction. Pray to God the driver would make for the Fairclough Foundation and safety and Charlotte would not be implicated in any way. He cursed himself anew for allowing her to come and reached for the fellow with some sort of a hook in his hands.

Minutes later he knew he would not last much longer, the energy needed to fight off this many taking its toll and his leg was howling in pain. A shadow of dark fell with a suddenness that was surprising and he was on the floor, three men on top of him, one with his hands clasped tightly about his throat.

Kicking out his left leg, he felt a connection with one assailant's temple and the man lay still. But then a bar of steel flashed down, crashing against his jaw, the pain so strong he could barely breathe.

If this is it, he thought, relaxing into the coming of death, then please, please let Charlotte be safe.

The banging on the carriage door was startling and one of the two footmen inside opened it. Harriet almost fell in, her eyes drenched in tears and her pallor deadly white.

'It is you, Lottie?'

She began to cry properly as she was hauled into Lottie's arms and before she knew it there was movement and the carriage was travelling in the opposite direction to which it had come. Homewards and as fast a speed as the horses could muster.

'Stop.' Lottie beat on the roof with as much force as she could manage and within a moment it came to a standstill, the driver at the window.

'Mr King said if there was anything untoward we were to make for home, miss. He said no exceptions.'

'Let me out. He needs help.' Her voice was stern and the man was silenced.

'I think it was you he wanted protected, Miss Fairclough.'

'No.' She stood and removed her cloak, unbuttoning the dress which she wore so that it fell away from her neck and loosening her hair. She also lifted her glasses from her bag and adjusted them across her nose so that the broken arm felt more comfortable. She needed to see properly to help Jasper and vainness would only hinder her.

'Was he hurt, Harriet? The man who saved you?'

'Not yet, but he will be. These are dangerous men to cross.'

'How many?'

'More than six or seven at my count, but I think Mr Carvall himself will not have stayed.'

'Come with me,' she said to the bulkiest of the footmen, wanting the other to stay here to protect Harriet. 'Can you fight?'

'Yes, ma'am. I were brought up in Whitechapel, so I am handy with my fists.'

'Good.'

She then reached in for the leash and extracted the dog. The mongrel would be a useful addition for the task she needed to complete. 'Follow me. You wait here, Harriet, and do not move.'

Harriet began to cry again and Lottie thought she was starting to think a lot like Jasper, understanding exactly what it felt like to be frightened for the safety of another.

They moved quickly towards the tavern, pushing open the door only a few moments later.

Jasper was down, lying prostrate but still conscious. His face was twisted in pain, his leg on an angle that was unusual. As the man above him grabbed a knife the dog suddenly pulled away, leaping across the wide space and crashing directly into the assailant's chest, knocking him back against the mantel. The heavy *thunk* of his skull sounded out and then he lay still.

Another man rounded on them now, larger than the last, but less dangerous somehow.

'Giles. Giles.' The name came out of her mouth in a shriek and she ran across the room to lean down across Jasper. 'What have you done to him? What has happened? Where is his gold? His purse? Where did you put it?'

That question had the man searching around and the footman next to her struck him before he realised his mistake.

Now there were five men on the floor and Jasper. The dog was licking his face and he stared at her in amazement, but there were still onlookers and the ruse would need to be completed before they were safe.

'If you come here one more time, Giles Hardy, I will have you hanged, drawn and quartered.' Her accent was that of the Rookery, all furious shrieking and righteous anger. It was so very easy to switch into the dialects of her childhood and she knew the moment that the people not directly involved relaxed. 'I have told you again and again, Husband, that I will not have it and still you wander. Well, this is the very last time, mark my words, and if it ever happens again there will be hell to pay.'

No one watching such a scene wanted to be involved in a complex domestic argument, especially when the wife was a harridan and the man she was haranguing was largely unresponsive.

'Bring him.'

She turned to the footman and watched as he raised Jasper, going to his other side when he was upright and helping him stand.

The blood in his right eye worried her, but for now she needed the illusion of exasperation and an end of patience. The dog followed them out, its hackles raised and growling all the way to the door.

Untouchable.

She took the first corner and turned it, leaning Jasper against the wall and speaking with the footman.

'Get the carriage. Come to that street there.'

It was a wider throughway and she hoped he would be quick. This part of the whole situation was probably the most dangerous because Carvall and his men had time to regroup if they were going to and the tavern was still awfully close.

The dog helped, though, his bristly growling presence a deterrent to anyone who might venture towards them.

Jasper opened his eyes just as the man left them.

'Hell.' He could barely say this as his lip was split.

'Will you ever listen, Charlotte?' His eyes swept across the alley in much the same way as the dog's, wary and distrustful. 'Did Harriet find you?'

'Yes, she is in the carriage and it is coming.'

The dog had crouched at his feet, though it held an air of menace even like that, its teeth easily seen in the half-light. Bared back and ready.

'Where will it come to?'

'There.' She pointed to the next corner and Jasper straightened. 'Can you walk?'

'Just. Heel,' he said to the dog as it sprang forward and the animal slunk into position behind him, tail down and head up. In this light there was blood on the animal's back right leg, she could see the glistening wet in the whiteness of fur. The hound had been hurt and badly, but she could not stop to examine the injury. He would have to take his chances just like them and survive until they found safety. It was the only way forward.

Jasper could not believe what had just happened. He had been rescued from certain death by Miss Charlotte Fairclough, who looked like a poorly dressed prostitute, the mangy, feral half-breed dog and his footman sporting a swollen eye that would be well blackened come the morning.

When he dropped his hand he felt a warm wet mouth lick at his fingers.

An unlikely rescue party with surprisingly effective tactics. Charlotte had turned the place upside down with her rendition of a hard-done-by wife who was only in the tavern to drag her errant husband back home and he had seen the dog leap across him when the ruffian had drawn his weapon.

He'd taken a risk by coming alone, but he'd known if he'd brought others Carvall would never have let him close. This way Harriet had been lured in as well, a minion offering sex for money to a new patron with a heavy purse of gold.

When the carriage pulled up they got in, the enormous dog slinking to the floor, and then they were off, through the streets of London towards the Foundation, Harriet's shaking sobs the only noise inside.

He could not believe she had come and saved him, Charlotte Fairclough with her wild hair curling and her whisky eyes shining. She had removed her broken glasses now, tucking them back into her generous bag.

'We did it. You are safe, Harriet. We will never let them take you again.' Her voice sounded measured, though he could also hear the shaking within it.

That brought a greater bout of crying. 'It were me, miss. I was the one who went freely in the first place on the promise of more money and a better life. No one took me, but then I realised the mistake of it all and they would not let me go either.'

'Is the laundry involved in all of this, Miss White?'

He felt Charlotte stiffen at his question and waited for an answer.

'I think it must be, sir. Mr Carvall has taken other girls from there, too, and I think Frank Wilkes knows about it because he said nothing, but I saw money pass through his hands.'

'So Wilkes is not only a coward, but a cheat as well.' Jasper snarled this.

Lottie sat forward, a heavy frown across her brow. 'My goodness, and we have been sending him young girls for work there for all of a year now.'

'How many?'

'Five, perhaps. Did you see any of the others, Harriet, when you were with Carvall?'

'No one, Miss Fairclough. Just me. I have seen and done things that make me crawl with the shame of it and now I do not know how I can ever fit back in.'

'You do it one breath at a time, one step at a time.' Jasper answered this because he had done exactly the same and he wanted to give the girl strength. Charlotte looked at him as if he had grown angel wings and a halo, her smile wide. 'I know because that is how I survived, too.'

Three hours later, having had something to eat and drink, Lottie sat with Jasper in the small family dining room at the back of the Foundation, a fire burning in the grate. Harriet had been dispatched to a bedroom to sleep, Claire watching over her to make certain she was not distressed and just for this moment the world was a fine one. Harriet had been restored to her rightful place and Jasper looked far less in agony than he had appeared before. The dog lay across his boots, fully stretched into the heat, his injured leg bound.

'He looks as though he is attached to you.' She pointed to the animal and its dark eyes opened.

'Mongrels are clever and they know a good lark to hold on to when they see one.'

'So you will keep him?'

'Isn't there some Chinese saying that states if someone saves your life you owe them a life? I imagine it applies to dogs as well.'

She laughed at that and thought that this was what happiness was, this moment, right here in conversation with Jasper.

'You should have stayed in the carriage, Charlotte, safely tucked away from the violence. If you'd been hurt…'

'But I wasn't.'

'Which was only by a stroke of luck.' He wiped back a lock of his hair with a hand that had every knuckle grazed. 'No one has ever put themselves at such risk for me before. If you hadn't come…'

'You did the same for me in Old Pye Street, Jasper.'

He looked up as she said his Christian name.

'I grant you that it was a clever ruse. I think the patrons of the Marquis of Granby tavern had no true direction in which to act. You softened the violence with a domestic spat and they were glad to see the back of us and sorry for us as well.'

'It's a trick I learned here at the Foundation. When you dampen down the stakes people tend to look the other way and are thankful that it is not them living in such a conundrum.'

'It must be a hard life, always helping those in trouble?'

She nodded. 'Sometimes it is, but it's also a good one.'

He looked exhausted tonight, his face sporting new bumps and bruises and his right arm held close to his body where it had been wrenched at the elbow.

'Thank you for getting Harriet out.'

He smiled, but she could tell that he wanted to ask her something. With patience she waited until he finally spoke.

'Would you come and have dinner with me tomorrow night at my town house? I can bring you back here afterwards.'

'It would be just us?' She knew this could not be something a single woman should do.

'Only if you wanted it to be.'

'I do.'

He nodded, for the first time a sort of uncertainty evident. 'I thought you might refuse.'

'Why?'

'Because alone and away from the Foundation I would hope I can kiss you again and I think you would know that.'

Warmth suffused the room and, as though aware of the undercurrents, the dog looked up and whined.

'Hero. Cease.'

'You will call him that? Hero.'

'Do you like it?'

'It suits him.'

This building held all the remnants of her family,

of Silas, of her parents and sister, of helping others, of business and compassion. She could well understand why Jasper wanted her to be at his town house, for it was a quieter space where there would be no interruptions, though she also thought of Meghan's visit the other day and frowned.

What would it mean to go there alone? Each time he had kissed her thus far they had only ever stopped because of intrusions. What if there were none? She felt her cheeks warming and looked away, though she was sure Jasper had seen what she had tried to hide from him.

Anticipation. Eagerness.

She would write another letter to Mama tonight and tell her of the rescue of Harriet. She would couch the note in terms that would not bring Lilian running back to London for she hoped to buy some time here to see where this dinner tomorrow might lead them.

'I think we also need to investigate what is happening at the laundry, Charlotte. Did Rosa O'Brian ever say she'd been approached?'

So he was back to business now, a man who wanted answers about the day's happenings. 'No, but perhaps she wouldn't be. Approached, I mean, with her face.'

'She is still beautiful and there is no accounting for the tastes of those who seek something different.'

'You think Carvall is picking off the newcomers, then? Taking them before they settle in and offering them so much more.'

'Harriet said as much. An offer too good to be refused is usually too good to be believed as well.'

'But a girl of nineteen may not realise that?'

'Until it is too late.'

Lottie enjoyed talking to Jasper like this, every possibility mooted and a sort of shared understanding in the issues. She felt reassured at the way he joined clues together and came out with an explanation of a problem. Like her parents used to. It was heartening.

She wished the night could have gone on for ever, but it was late and when he stood the dog did, too.

'I shall send a carriage around at five in the afternoon tomorrow for you. I hope you sleep well.'

He did not step forward in any way and such restraint was touching. She had the sense that he wanted to wait till tomorrow when the fright of this night was further away and things had settled before he asked her for anything more. One of the Fairclough Foundation servants came in to show him out, the dog following him, and when he had gone it felt as if all the air and light had left the room.

Crossing to the window, she watched him step into his carriage, a slight flare of light showing his face as the conveyance moved forward and then he was lost in the blackness.

Chapter Eleven

All day she had been nervous. She had spent the morning with Harriet in a house in Clapham, for she knew there was a job as a scullery maid on offer there. Harriet was given the position and, thankfully, it was one where she could start immediately.

'I need to get back to normal, Lottie, and this will help me do that. I have always enjoyed being in a kitchen, so this is just perfect. Besides, it's a good distance from the Rookery. I doubt anyone will know me here so it will be a new start and I will take it one breath at a time just as Mr King said it and survive.'

'But you will come and see me at the Foundation?'

'Of course I will and I cannot thank you both enough for what you have done for me. I was foolish, I know it, terribly foolish, but I shall never be so again.'

When Lottie reached home again just after twelve she pampered herself, having a bath in the afternoon, something she had never done before, and shampooing her hair with a special concoction of lavender and lemon.

Claire, her maid, had stopped haranguing her. She was now simply delighted by Mr King and extolled all his virtues.

'Your papa would have liked him, Miss Lottie. He is man of his word and the help he gave to Harriet in her hour of need was beyond wonderful. I am glad he is taking you to dinner at his sister's house tonight because Mrs Gibson seems a very nice woman and kind with it.'

'I shall make sure to tell him of your good opinion, Claire.'

She hated to lie, but felt in the circumstances it would be easier.

As Claire held out a towel the clock in the corner rang out the hour of two.

'Goodness, is that the time already? I need to dry my hair and find something to wear. I was thinking of my navy gown, the one with the lace that Amelia gave me last year.'

It had the lowest bodice of all her gowns and Lottie thought she might as well use the assets she had. Such a thought was daring and bold, but after yesterday she felt different, more certain of her direction and less inclined to sit back and wait until life came to her.

In all her twenty-two years it had not and neither had it done so for Amelia. The men she'd met through the Fairclough Foundation were good upstanding gentlemen who had often expressed interest of varying degrees, but none of them had made her heart beat faster or her breath come in gulps.

As Jasper did.

Part of her wished Millie was here to talk with and part of her was glad she was at the Malverlys'. She would have liked to ask about why her sister's relationship with Jasper had ended and what she had thought of him. She knew her brother had always liked him so that was one member of the family who would be in her corner.

A mirror to one side of the room caught her reflection and she stiffened. She had never been a thin girl, her curves as much a part of her as her wild and curling hair. For the first time ever she wondered if a man would find her attractive without her clothes on. She clenched her teeth together. My goodness, could she really be thinking of doing this, of allowing Jasper to know her truly? Another thought struck her, though, straight after that one. A kiss might be all he wanted. After all, he was a man born and raised into a family of good name and fortune.

All of this thinking was just confusing her. Should she even go to his town house alone and put herself into this position? She had known him for only a matter of days. Hardly any time at all. And yet…

She'd always been so good at taking her chances and here she was second-guessing herself and overthinking.

Tonight would be what it would be.

This thought made her happier and stronger and

with resolve she walked across to her wardrobe and took out the navy gown.

She loved him. She did. She loved Jasper with every fibre of her body and with her whole heart and, if nothing else came from this save a kiss, she would always be grateful for the knowledge that he could engender such feelings in her and that she had reached out for her own infinite possibilities in life.

She was certain that Nanny Beth would be up there in Heaven cheering her on.

Charlotte Fairclough was here. His carriage had just arrived, the fire was warming the front salon and he had chilled wine on the sideboard.

His leg was quiet tonight.

Jasper smiled at the description, but he had always thought of the pain in a gradient of noise, quiet to howling. After the fight yesterday he had imagined he might awake to a far worse ache and had been pleasantly surprised to know silence.

He hoped she had not brought her maid or a servant to oversee her visit under the guise of a chaperon. His sister had asked him this morning about Charlotte Fairclough and her movements and he had been as evasive as he could, for the last thing he wanted was for Meghan to call in uninvited again.

Lord. He had seldom considered things like this before, always being so certain of his movements. Charlotte Fairclough's bravery last night had sent him spinning, her reckless disregard for her own safety lending a layer of disbelief and incredulity. He could never have imagined any woman of his acquaintance being so bold. Verity had absconded at the first sign of trouble, leaving him in a hole so deep he still wondered exactly how he had managed to extricate himself.

The front door opened and he heard the softness of her voice asking his man a question. About a painting, he thought, and sought to imagine which one she had had an interest in.

His mother, perhaps. Her other-worldly beauty always intrigued anyone new to her portrait. The dog cocked his head and listened, tail wagging.

Then the door opened and she was there.

'Thank you for coming.'

His words sounded formal, but at that particular moment it was the best he could come up with. She looked young, absurdly young and scared, a beautiful girl wrapped in a navy dress that had seen better days, her hair once again fraying at its tethers.

'Would you like a drink?'

Her eyes shifted across to the wine and she nodded. 'Just a small glass, please.'

Perhaps because she didn't want any loss of control? He did as she asked and deposited a half-filled glass in her hand.

'It is Chateau Lafite from the vineyards outside the village of Pauillac in the Medoc region of France. The King's Wine, it is called by many, and the vintage of 1798 was one of their very finest.' He was talking now to fill in the gap, even though he knew she'd hardly be interested in all the peculiarities of the wine.

She drank it quickly and then placed the glass down on the table beside her without giving any opinion. He did not offer more.

'How is Miss White this morning?'

'I took her to meet her new employer and the woman was kind. I think it will be a perfect place for her.'

'To forget?'

'Precisely.'

'And survive?'

Funny, this shortened way of speaking between them. He'd felt it before with her.

'It is lucky your mother has such capable hands to leave the running of the Fairclough Foundation in.'

At that she looked up.

'It is lonely sometimes.' This was said in a tone that one might use in church. 'Good works do not leave much time for friends or for going out or for the wasting of hours.'

'Time being of the essence in the saving of way-ward souls?'

'You are laughing at me?'

He shook his head, taking her hand as he stepped forward. A small hand without adornment, fingers slender and still. She did not snatch it away, a fact that heartened him.

'Not laughing. Harriet will need time to come to terms with what she has lost and when she stops look-ing over her shoulder and turns to gaze ahead, then she will live again.'

'Was it like that for you? After your accident?'

'It was.'

'She told me that now she feels she is ruined for ever.'

'She is young, Charlotte, and for ever is a very long time.'

His thumb ran in a circle on the inside of her palm. Distracting her. She wanted to let the words go and clasp on to him, tightly, the wine settling in her stomach with warmth, a wine that was different from any she had ever tasted before.

But he'd moved back and the next second a servant appeared, wheeling a small table into the room, food laden on its top.

'The cook has made a selection of things to begin with. I did not know the food you favoured so she has made an array to suit differing tastes.' He placed two dining chairs at the table and pulled one out for her.

Lottie sat on one side and Jasper on the other, but the table was so small she could have still reached across to touch him.

'I have been doing some asking around about Mr Carvall, and it seems as if he is a man who disappears often. But I found Frank Wilkes in the Rookery this afternoon and threatened him with taking all I know of his part in this to the police unless he helps us.'

'How?'

'I have asked him to set up another meeting with Carvall at the laundry and to let me know of the timings. I will take my own men with me when he does and I have sweetened the deal with a good amount of gold.'

'Do you think you can trust him? Wilkes?'

He shook his head. 'No, he is a pimp who has traded young women for gain, so I doubt he is going to be the sort who suddenly discovers a moral compass. But if the meeting is at the laundry then at least I know the place and the surroundings. Twigg will back me up, too.'

Charlotte felt sick. He'd twice been beaten by those associated with Carvall and a third attempt at uncovering the prostitution ring set around Old Pye Street seemed even more dangerous than the last two.

'Perhaps we should just go to the constabulary with the facts we have already?'

'And let those involved escape to start all over again, somewhere else? You would want that?'

This meeting had gone off on a tangent somehow, all the danger derailing her calm. Now fear shrank the hope she had arrived with and the kiss she had been thinking of faded into the distance.

'I want you to be safe,' she said. The bruises on his face were so easily seen this evening and his arm was bandaged. 'I don't want you hurt any more.'

'Hell, I could be saying the same to you for wandering these parts of a dangerous London always alone. If Carvall did not see you there at the Marquis of Granby tavern playing your ruse as the furious wife, then others will certainly remember you and it won't be long till they put your face and that of the Foundation together. And then what? How can you protect yourself?'

'Do you think things like this have not happened before? Do you think it's easy dealing with people at the end of their wits clutching to the last shreds of their existence?'

Frustration made the words louder than she had meant them.

'Which is exactly why your brother should not have hived off, leaving three women alone to cope.' He shook his head. 'And now it's just you, Charlotte, with disrepute and lawlessness at your doorstep and no true defence in which to rebuff it.'

'Save for you?' She had finally grasped the main thread of his argument and her heart sank.

'Exactly.'

They were left facing each other over a roomful of questions, caught in the crossfire of a gang warfare and a lucrative prostitution racket. The food felt dry in her mouth as Lottie reached for some lemon water.

It was true what he said. The Fairclough Foundation lay unprotected, all her father's dreams eroded by a present danger that had arisen from nowhere and they had little personal money left to try to rebuff the threat.

Their only shield was Jasper.

Was it worth it?

That thought had her breath hitching, the terror in her heart changing into sheer and utter surprise. Always she had fought for the ideals of the Foundation and spent every moment of her working life thinking of how they might help the women in need who came to them. Yet now with Jasper's life balanced in this way she was no longer certain that she did not wish to simply quit the whole thing and leave. Leave her mother and father's dream to find her own.

'Perhaps I would like one more small glass of wine.'

He poured her exactly the same measure as he had the last time.

'It was easier when Papa was alive, the Foundation and its running, but lately things have become a lot more difficult.'

'Because of your brother's absence?'

'Silas wasn't altogether happy about being stuck here, which is why he moved to work in Liverpool and then America. He wanted to forge his own pathway, find his own life, I suppose.'

'And you, Charlotte. What is it you want?'

'To be happy. I want the Foundation to be as it was once, a proper home, like this one is for you.'

At that he laughed and looked around. 'It's more of a family heirloom than a home. Mine to watch over and pass on. I haven't stayed in it much. I haven't stayed anywhere much.'

The hound now lay beside him sleeping, a study of loyal admiration as Jasper's fingers ran across soft brown ears.

When he saw where she was looking he smiled. 'I think this dog suits me. Certainly he is well up for a fight. How was it you got him?'

'Someone dumped him in the river. His legs were

tied and because he was such a big dog the man who saved him was not able to keep him. He would have cost too much to feed, so he brought him to us.'

'The Foundation deals in abused dogs now, too, then?'

She laughed. 'Mama was not pleased, but Amelia was on my side and they were off to the country party the next day.'

'Your sister was kind. I remember that.'

'I always wondered why you did not stay around to get to know her better?' Lottie hated the way she had asked this, a curiosity in her voice that was not becoming. Stiffening, she waited for his answer.

'She was a dutiful girl, but I prefer recklessness and the ability to be brave.'

He was speaking of her.

'I like a woman who knows her mind and goes after the things she thinks are important, no matter how difficult the situation might be.'

The air seemed to change around them, hidden things revealed in light. She felt the hairs on her arms rise into thrall.

'My family often say that I am highly impetuous and very stubborn.'

'Then all the better for it.'

He had risen from his seat now and she did the same, one of his fingers tracing the line of her cheek and running in a single stroke across her upper lip.

She shivered.

'When you arrived at the tavern with your hair undone, your dress unbuttoned and with a story so absurd it could only be believable, I thought no one could have risked their own life for mine like you did. Spectacularly.'

'It was a mutual thing. You were there to save Harriet, a stranger you didn't even know. I could hardly do otherwise.'

He breathed out, both his hands now around her arms holding her still.

'But that is where I beg to differ, Charlotte. You could have left in the carriage and never looked back. You could have sent in the footmen and waited with Harriet, but you did not.' He frowned, the line between his eyes deepening. 'I am not an easy man. I am not a man filled with altruism or philanthropy. I am damaged and impaired and I am not even sure if...'

'Shh.' She leaned forward and took his mouth with hers, felt him move, felt him take in breath, felt the heat rise and slam into desire.

Jasper was so new to her and yet there was something about him that was known. She'd often felt alone in her life, but in his company she did not, she simply felt whole and perfect, so when one hand entwined around the back of her neck she went gladly.

What was it about Charlotte Fairclough that made him lose all good sense and logic? He should be limiting his reactions and slowing down, but he could not, his mouth slanting against hers and changing the angles so that they were closer, joined, bound into something that was both ancient and new.

He'd never felt like this before, caught between the lines with a woman he could not quite work out. His tongue moved, a need mirrored in his body, hardness forming, nothing hidden as the same desperation he'd felt before rose, the world spiralling away into just here and now.

'Hell, Charlotte.' Her eyes snapped open. 'I don't know if I can stop.'

He had to tell her, had to let her know. Had to allow her the choice of not just a kiss.

'Then don't.'

Her words were soft, whispered, ragged, borne on the edge of her own need, her golden eyes melting into darkness.

And just like that it was easy, taking her to him, finding her centre, knowing her warmth and her sweetness. A certain truth.

For all his life Jasper had been running towards something and away from something else. But here he was stopped, still, at a final destination. Like James Bruce on that small hillock that signified the undiscovered source of the Blue Nile in Ethiopia. Like Captain James Cook in the Pacific, finding places he had always only just imagined. Every adventure book he'd ever read and loved had that final knowledge of an arrival and it felt like that here, in the drawing room of his town house on Arlington Street on the edge of Green Park in Piccadilly. With Charlotte Fairclough.

Home was not the sole domain of a building. No, home was also possible in a person, the right person, the one who would not falter or crumble or disappoint or disappear. He felt her tongue caress his own, their mouths wide now, tasting and knowing, nothing held back or concealed.

Moving her against the wall, his hands resting on each side, he took in a breath and felt her do the same. She was trapped, in his care, watching him with her swollen lips and flushed face and a pulse that beat like a drum in her neck, her nipples as hard as cherries as he reached out and touched.

'Beautiful.' His voice was deep and he cleared his throat, one hand pushing back the thick blue wool and finding cambric. His mouth fastened over the fabric, the wet of it sticking, pale pink skin darkening under the caress.

Her head tilted backwards and she said his name, mindless and repeated. She was like a vessel waiting for him to fill, all new and ready. Her curves were surprising. She always looked so small in her clothes buttoned up over flesh, but here the abundance of her breasts drove him on. He felt the weight of them in his hands and bent again to suckle, pulling the cambric clear so that it was skin against skin, her nipple budding in response.

'Hold me here.' He placed her palm against his face and sucked harder, no longer gentle, and her fingers clenched against his cheek, her breast rising in his mouth.

'More.' Her order now, whispered and throaty.

His teeth closed down so that she took in breath, waiting, and the sharp edge to his lust was so foreign it made him feel lightheaded.

Like a young boy, green to it all, unable to slow down, whorls of need drawn on her skin, the porcelain white lost into a mounting urgency, passion filling all the cracks of his more usual caution.

'My God, Charlotte.'

He drew back, her breast naked in the light, and she made no move at all to cover herself, instead watching him, her whisky eyes dazed and glassy, a stamp of her lust drawn in around desire.

So beautiful that he almost wept.

He lifted the fabric of her gown back, covering the bounty, draping it into modesty. Her hair fell about her shoulders in riotous curls, the colours of brown and gold and a deeper amber all mixed into one.

Yet still she did not move, did not rouse herself into the ordinary, her breath fast, her tongue wetting her lips and her neck a thin stretched column of white.

Laying one finger across the pulse, he listened, the beat far faster than her stillness might have relayed, her own want as ripe as his.

The deep throb of his arousal was worrying, unappeased and pressing. He must not go further. He could not take her like this, unpromised and a virgin likely to boot, on the floor of his unlocked front salon, a dozen servants roaming the house.

God, what had he been thinking? Turning away, he poured himself a brandy, drinking the lot in one long swallow and pouring the next.

She merely watched him, all words gone, but talking with her body. Like a temptress. Like a siren, unpractised but fatal. The emptiness in him surfaced fully and he could not help anger.

'Your brother would kill me should I go further. Dress yourself.'

When she didn't he turned, a hand running through his hair, the room alight with intention.

Then she leant against the wall behind her as if to find a balance. There was something in her stance that was sensual and lustful and covetous. Something innocent, too. A sacrificial lamb came to mind and he pushed the thought away.

No recriminations and so very easy.

And what then?

Lust was simple. It was what came next that was harder and if she stayed around she would know him soon as he knew himself, wandering the corridors sleepless, screaming with the pain, only a few years of true mobility left if he was lucky and less if he was not. A half-man filled with bitterness, a shadow man who had so long been out of the light.

But she was not finished and it was that which undid him for she simply pulled her bodice off her shoulders, the thin straps of her petticoat falling with the navy wool until there were only her breasts beckoning him and calling him home.

A brave and bold move, the light in her eyes telling him that she understood what she offered, the implications and the complications.

'I want you, Jasper.'

Impetuous. Stubborn. Reckless. All the things her

family had called her and counting against him here. Unchangeable.

He touched the red whorl on the rise of one breast, his mark, his brand, waiting for denial or panic. Neither came. She was true to her word and he took in breath.

'And after?' He had to say it, had to make her realise all that he might not be able to promise.

'Then I will know.'

She didn't say more and for that he was glad. The knowledge of intercourse? The knowledge of pain? The knowledge of anger or the knowledge of guilt?

She'd come into this without any promise of for ever. She had not even asked him for it. She had brought her body and her braveness and she laid it before him in a way that took courage. So bloody much of it he was wordless.

'Not here in this room.' That much he did know. Not here in a place where interruption was certain. He lifted the drooping neckline of her gown again back in to place. He could do nothing to tame her hair, the curls floating like an unbridled siren about her head.

Jasper would throw her out? He would bundle her off in his carriage without dressing her properly? He would refuse to quench the fire of her want without even stopping to tell her why?

She pulled back, a flame of anger snaking through the utter certainty of her path and felt the wool of the gown scratch against the nakedness of her breasts even as his hand against her back shepherded her on.

Not to the front door after all, but up a staircase, with myriad portraits looking down upon them, dark stern faces from the past. Breathing in, she made herself relax, made herself fluid, reaching for the anticipation, the hope and the promise. The beat of lust had returned and she relished it.

She was twenty-two and she knew what she wanted. A crossroads, a choice. She could not go back. She wanted Jasper as she had never wanted anyone before, she wanted to hold him, know him, taste him and feel him moving within her. She wanted to be formless and boneless and spent.

In less than a day she would be back to the rules of ordinary life, the conventions of the altruistic, the expectations of goodness, the contracts of the Foundation in all their forms of servitude. After this any chance at something different would be gone and she would be who she had always been, dutiful, restless and lonely.

His chamber was enormous, the dark burgundy velvet across the bed catching the light of candle and that of flame burning in the grate. Near the window sat two large leather chairs and a mahogany desk piled with books and notes.

A perfect setting. She stood and watched him, her mouth dry. She wished he might just come across and take the clothes from her and carry her to his bed like the heroes in the clandestine romances her sister had gathered. The wine was wearing off, too, the warmth in her stomach clotting into fear.

Would he hurt her? Did it hurt? Would there be blood?

She pushed those thoughts away and smiled because if he saw her fear he would leave. She knew it.

'You are brave, Charlotte.'

His words were soft.

'I am here of my own accord, Jasper. There is only that courage in it.'

'Have you lain with anyone else?'

She wanted to nod and tell him yes, but she knew that there were ways a body could refute such an untruth and so she didn't. Instead she said nothing and saw his concern.

'If you are virgin, then it may be painful.'

She turned away and the words stopped. Unfastening her hair, she felt the heaviness of curls come loose. A suitable answer. Dramatic. Unconventional. Theatrical.

Then she hitched up her skirt and turned back.

No longer questions. A line had been drawn. She saw how his gaze drank in her breasts and her thighs and the soft line of her hips and knew then that she had him. He was a man, after all, and surely there were limits on self-control.

'If you are untutored, you can tell me to stop at any time and I will. I promise.'

Long limits, then. Far longer than the men she often came into contact with at the Foundation through the women who had been abused by them.

But she believed him and it became easier again.

'I want…everything.' The fear had left altogether

now, desire filling in caution. 'Your sister said you have had many women who wanted you. She said you treat women well and that you know how to make them happy. Nanny Beth said that with a good man there is fulfilment and contentment in the bedroom and she said that if you were lucky there is more.'

'More?'

She blushed, not wanting to mention love. This was love on her behalf and lust on his, but for now it was what she would settle for. She loved him enough for the both of them. She loved him so completely that it hurt.

He was damaged and lonely and fearful and broken, but she could try to fix him and make him understand the love that she felt. She wanted him to know that lust was only a pathway to something better if it was done perfectly, without expectation and demand, without repayment or compensation.

Two halves to make a whole. The cleaving of souls. The last honesty and the perfect redemption. This is what they would understand together tonight. She prayed for it to be such even as she spoke.

'Lust holds its own liberty, Jasper.'

When he frowned she wondered if he understood things quite as well as she'd hoped.

Chapter Twelve

If she believed that, then she was a virgin. The girls whose amorous interludes had produced a child came to mind, women and men caught in webs that neither wanted, expectations leaving them shackled. Hardly liberty.

He'd never fathered a child because he was unfailingly careful, the lamb intestine condoms he favoured softened with lye and sulphur. The fashion was to use such barriers to counter disease, but he had always used it for control, the horror of an unplanned birth making him fastidious about protection. Freedom was a choice that was important to him and, save for the debacle with Verity, he'd never given it up. Seen from his perspective now, he thought he must have been delusional at that time and that his escape from a marriage with a woman like her had been a lucky one.

Charlotte was a different kettle of fish altogether. She held courage and honesty and integrity. With her skin mellowed gold against flame and candlelight she was an innocent Venus asking to be deflowered.

That thought brought his blood up, heated in her acquiescence. I want everything, she had said, and his erection rose beneath the superfine of his trousers. He did not wish to frighten her as he reached out, knowing the bounty of one breast and then the other, feeling his way.

He thought she might move or falter, but she didn't, rather she stood there watching him, her breathing hitching as his touch strayed lower. He waited again for denial, but all he got was a softening. Her legs opened and she smiled at him.

'God.' He couldn't help it. 'God help me, Charlotte, but you are the most beautiful woman I have ever seen.'

The wrong words because her eyes darkened and for the first time she flinched.

'You don't believe me. Let me show you, then. Here,' he whispered and ran his finger over the curve of her hip, loosening the blue wool from its tether so that it fell around her feet. The cambric petticoat was all that was left now, drunkenly attached by a few small buttons to her waist.

'Like a goddess sent down from the heavens by Zeus himself. Aphrodite, perhaps, the goddess of love and persuasion.'

'A tall order,' she returned, but smiled. 'For every man who looked upon her saw his own ideal standard of beauty reflected back.'

'I rest my case,' he responded and his hand rose

to her face, his finger running across her cheekbone and the line of her nose. 'You have read the ancient Grecian myths, then?'

'Often. I also liked the book you sent me.'

'There are others you might enjoy.' His voice was husky and low. 'I had a friend who translated an ancient Indian text for me in parts. Within such writing the forbidden was illuminated and the rules of desire were enlightened.'

'Tell me one.' She licked her lips as she said this. No artifice or pretence. No chance for him to misunderstand exactly what she was saying. She had arrived at this point with an equality that startled her, the power on both sides revealing. Jasper was not a man given to façade and she was the same.

When he began to speak she was surprised by the content.

"'Lovers, blinded by passion, in the friction of sexual battle, are caught up in their fierce energy and pay no attention to danger.'"

'Is it that? Dangerous?' The very thought made her warmer.

'It can be.'

'And you are well versed in such practices?'

Shadow came into his eyes. 'I am not a saint, Charlotte.'

'And I do not wish you to be, Jasper.'

His finger came around her lips and opened her mouth. She tasted the salt on him and knew a quick jolt of pleasure.

'When one makes love there is a preamble, an

overture to set the tone of it.' He withdrew his finger and licked it, the wet of her mouth glistening on his lips. 'A sharing that is so intimate only lovers can understand the detail.'

She felt her heart beat in her throat, a peculiar vulnerability that she never wanted to end. Lovers. Even the word was daring.

'Open your mouth for me.'

She did and he came inside, not gently but with a force that caught her out, his tongue now where his finger had been, probing, asking, finding in his insistence a response from her. Her head tipped back and her breath simply stopped as she allowed him all he wanted. Not easy, not quiet, but invasive and stimulating all at the same time.

This was a different kiss from any he had given her before because it stamped another power into the act. When she moved he stilled her and when he broke away finally his hand curved around the column of her neck.

'Lovemaking is as much in the mind as it is in the body, Charlotte. Can you feel what I am telling you?'

'You want to own me.' It wasn't a question.

He smiled. 'Just for now. Later there will come a time when you will rule me and I promise you that your control can be as absolute as mine.'

A further troth wrapped in the sensual. She could barely breathe with the thought of it.

'Open your legs. Let me in.'

No intermediate step between this and a kiss. Shocked, she allowed it and his hand fell to the skin between her thighs and then rose, up into the wet warmth of her, pushing forward gently till the thickness hurt.

'The last barrier between innocence and the forbidden knowledge,' he said in triumph.

She was not embarrassed as he felt her, his eyes watching and daring her to look away.

'The hidden treasure, the final breaching, but not yet, my love.'

His endearment was surprising, but then she thought all men probably whispered such words in the throes of sexual passion and he would be no different.

His hand retreated and came up to her mouth again, the taste of herself offered back.

'Lick me and know yourself, Charlotte. The elixir of life.'

She did so, the musk of sex arousing, the forbiddenness of it wondrous and the hard truth of his offering making her groan with the want for more.

Nothing so far was as she thought it would be. He had not thrown her down and mounted her, a few pushes and a finish. It was what the women at the Foundation spoke of when they thought she was not listening, the mundane tediousness of an act that just caused them problems.

Here she could only feel the enchantment, an edge of danger adding to the illusion, pleasure and thrill in equal proportion. Every fibre of her body yearned for more.

It would hurt, she knew it would, but she wanted that pain as much as she wanted the pleasure. He had shown her this so simply that she no longer felt afraid.

But he had not finished, his hands moving to her breasts now and cradling them, weighing them, holding them up so that flesh spilled across his hands.

'Heaven on earth can be found between a woman's breasts.' He tweaked one nipple. 'Men dream of living here, caught between the swell of life and birth.'

His mouth fastened on one nipple and he sucked, his other fingers kneading the opposite nipple so that she was lost in sensation.

She wanted him fiercely and violently, inside her. She wanted what those books talked of, a sudden and explosive taking, ferocious in its passion, intense and powerful.

When he raised his head she saw the knowledge in his eyes, too.

'Now you are ready.'

Lifting her, he removed the last of her clothes, the fall of the cambric adding to her desperation and the brown in his eyes was glowing in need.

The bed was soft and the velvet beneath naked skin felt sinful. As far from the Fairclough Foundation as she had ever been and she only wanted to go further.

Unbuttoning the fall of his trousers he fitted a small sheath across the top of his manhood, stretching down the edges.

'For safety,' he said.

His boots were kicked off next and then he was across her, leaning over, nudging her thighs into position and readying himself.

Tipping her chin up, he made her look at him, his gaze promising a truth that was undeniable. He would have her. Now.

She nodded and he came in, not slowly, but with one long hard stroke and stopped as the pain flared around them, the throb of a last resistance, the intake of breath and the coinciding retreat of her own body.

'No. Stay still. It will pass.'

He did not let her move an inch, but lay there with her, holding in the ache, stifling it with his heat, the thickness of him cradled inside.

And then he moved again, but slightly, so that the flesh was gentled, a new sensation arising from the old.

A question, a beginning, a warmth that grew into a need to move with him, fast and furious, the slick wetness sucking and the friction of his body holding the heat.

'Come with me,' he whispered so that the words were quiet. 'Come with me now, Charlotte. Let go and come. Now.'

And she did, the roiling waves of all he talked about upon her, the pain gone and the pleasure beaching from her toes to her head, the last shake of his ardour and then stillness. Pressed close together, both their hearts beating like drums in a matching rhythm.

She was elated. So this is what the books spoke of in their reverence and disbelief. This act. This totality. The completeness took her from this world to a far-off place where all she wanted was more. Docile.

Compliant. Submissive to a master lover who understood her body as no one else ever had.

Different. Changed. No longer an innocent. She smiled at the word.

Jasper swore under his breath and stayed still. God, the act of copulation had never felt like this, an undone longing and a certainty that had always been missing before.

He had hurt her, he knew it, even with his care.

The small death. The French were right. *La petite mort.* He took in a shaky breath and tried to gather himself.

Her eyes were closed and her breathing was light and shallow.

'Charlotte?'

A whisky-gold glance sharpened against his own. 'Yes?'

'You were magnificent.'

His arm rested across her, hand cupping her breast. It felt as if he was speaking through water, exhaustion snaking through the lateness of the day. And yet...

He took her nipple between his forefinger and his thumb and pressed down. It was not quite over and she had to understand that, too.

Her head turned, a frown across her forehead.

'I will take away the pain if you let me.'

'How?'

He came across her and for a second saw fright in her eyes.

'Not in that way. It is too soon. But in this one.'

One finger sought her swollen redness and then his tongue took over, licking at the nub of desire, finding exactly what he wanted.

She would come again, he knew it, but this time it would be easy and he would happily accommodate her need. He pushed in higher, his finger now moving across her nub.

'No.' She groaned this from above, trying to still him, but he took her hand and held it against her thigh while he worked, bent to his job.

He felt her release in the wavering vibrations. Small at first and then stronger so that her body clenched in reply and the breath she held was expired in gasps. His other hand now sat across her stomach, nursing the orgasm. And when it had finished she began to cry, soft sobs at first and then louder.

With worry he raised himself and turned, brushing away the tears on her cheeks.

'Are you hurt?' He was trying to understand it.

She shook her head, but would not look at him.

'Then what is it? Why do you cry?'

'Because…because… I loved it. Because I want it again. Because I have become a woman I barely recognise and no different from Harriet or the women who ply their trade in Old Pye Street. For coin for them maybe, but for me…for pleasure.'

Jasper fell back against the pillows and laughed in a way he never had in the bed of any woman before, with relief and with gladness and with an all-consuming liberation.

For an hour he had not thought of himself or his

injury or his tentative future. No, he had served Charlotte with as much finesse as he could and now she imagined herself a fallen woman. There was no sense in any of it.

'Pleasure is an underestimated virtue. Personally, I hold it right up there with truth and honesty.'

She smiled, the dimples on her cheeks small shadows of darkness.

'And any man would be thrilled to have a woman in his bed who thought as you do.'

She had crawled against him now, winding her legs around his. He felt her breath at his throat and the flutter of her eyelashes on the top of his arm where he held her. Outside the wind had risen and the rain was returned, a stinging freezing patter and further abroad the sound of thunder.

'I used to count the time between the lightning and thunder.' Her voice was quiet. 'But when Nanny Beth died I stopped doing it because she said it was wasting life to try to work out things that would change nothing. I think she was referring to my life really and giving me a push to find new pathways, other things.'

'Things like this?'

She laughed then and he thought he had not heard that sound often enough from her.

'I doubt this was quite the direction of her thoughts.'

A new bolt of lightning took away the darkness and if she did not count the seconds till the thunder came then he did.

'Five.' He said this out loud.

His finger ran across her nose as she nodded. He liked the way it turned up at the end, distinguishing hers from the more patrician noses now in fashion. Her lips turned up, too, at each end, a small indent emphasising them. Everything about her was different and charming. He wanted to keep Charlotte here in his bed for ever, away from the world, just the two of them lost in time and alone.

'Faced with the proposition of the vastness of the universe we probably know less than nothing. For all we discern the beats between lightning and thunder might be an undiscovered music.' Jasper's voice was low.

'Oh, I like that. A symphony in space that no one listens to.'

'Except for us.'

She turned and he felt her finger against his nipple and took in a breath. No woman had ever done that to him before, not even the practised courtesans he'd bedded at a place in Covent Garden in the throes of his addiction and ones that catered to each and every fantasy.

When her mouth fastened across him the shock burned its way to his toes.

'God.'

She looked up. 'You take the name of the Lord in vain too often, Mr King.' Then she returned to her work, her teeth now nipping, the pain slicing reality into shards of delight.

'Anyone who can lecture on the niceties of religious tenets while generating a lust without boundary has to be an original, Miss Fairclough.' He tried to move, but she kept him there under the pressure of her opened palm.

'My turn now. You did promise after all.'

Jasper breathed in, his do-gooding soul-saving lover presenting him with yet another example of the diversity of her gifts. He could barely believe the position he was in, lying here and waiting, his heart beating so fast and loud that he knew she must hear it and the sweat on his forehead building.

He never let others take control. He was always the one in the lead and, although he might have promised her this dominion over him earlier, he had not actually thought she would take him up upon the troth.

Swallowing, he made himself be still, counting the seconds of submissiveness beneath his breath in much the same way as he had the gap between lightning and thunder.

One second. Two seconds. Three seconds. Four seconds. Slowly. Deliberately. As if his life depended on such detachment.

And it did because even underneath regulation other capricious whims burst through the carefully constructed limit.

She was making him live again piece by piece, an unpractised virgin of godly persuasion who should in all truth have nothing to do with him.

But she played him like a maestro and when she pushed back the sheet from where it covered his right leg and ran her touch down his scar he nearly leapt from the bed with shock.

'I wish I had been there for you when this happened.'

He caught her hand to make her stop, his allowance of control strained and the honesty in her voice breaking him down altogether.

'And I am glad that you were not.'

'Because it was so terrible?'

He breathed in slowly. 'Sometimes I still use a stick. A mahogany stick with a silver handle and I hate it.'

'But it helps?'

'Yes.'

She watched him now, closely, the gold in her eyes fiery.

'Secrets are always hidden in the most unlikely of places, Jasper, but when they are shared their power is defused.'

'You really believe that?'

This time she blushed, a surprising thing in a woman so very candid.

'Perhaps not,' she answered at length. 'After this evening the secrets of the sensual are more powerful than I could have ever believed them to be.'

Her hand ran between his thighs, probing upwards.

'See,' she whispered. 'Not diluted, but magnified.'

His manhood had risen and as it brushed across her arm, he felt the softness of her skin there even as her fingers closed about it. Growing and wanting again.

He should reach for a condom, for he still had a couple in the drawer in the cabinet beside the bed, but a languid contentment had stolen across him and he

simply lay there as she sat and took him inside herself, moving up and down, quietly at first and then
faster. Then starlight burst within him and she tensed,
milking him with her orgasm, clenched around him
and riding the delight, a storm of feeling and submission, a maelstrom of power.

As she collapsed he took her in his arms and they
lay curled together, the clock in the corner beating
out the hour of nine.

It was late when she woke again, so late that even
the shadows held shadows and the thinness of time
was palpable. She lay turned towards him, their hands
clasped. Big hands. Capable hands. Hands that had
shown her things that she never knew existed. Wondrous things.

A glint of light told her that he was awake and
watching. Her.

'I sent a note to the Foundation and said that you
were at my sister's for the night. So that nobody would
worry.'

'When?' She had not felt him leave the bed.

'After ten.'

'What time is it now?'

'Just turned three. I heard the bells of St James's
a moment ago.'

She realised then that he was now dressed in one
of his fine linen shirts, the tail of it tucked around
his thighs.

'You have been up?'

The whiteness of his teeth showed in a smile. It

was quieter now and the storm had passed. When she listened there was nothing but silence.

'I want to give you something.'

She felt the rustle of sheets as he moved and then the small flare of a single candle on a side table banished the blackness.

He had pushed pillows behind him as a resting place and she sat, too, in the generous nest of them.

'This,' he said then and opened his hand. A small, long, green-velvet box sat on his palm, a golden catch on one side.

'I thought you should have had some jewellery the other night at the ball and you didn't.'

When she opened it, she saw a necklace finely wrought with stones of gold.

'They are topaz. They match your eyes. The necklace was my mother's.'

Emotion kept her speechless.

'I think they would look well upon you, Charlotte.'

He removed them from their box and fastened them around her neck. She felt the gold take up the warmth of her skin and her fingers ran across the line of the piece.

'This is beautiful.'

'Like you are.'

'And expensive.'

'I am wealthy.'

'Yet these are an heirloom.' She wanted to add the words 'for your wife when you marry', but this was too hard to say. As the silence lengthened Lottie could feel the tension of his thoughts.

'I would give you my whole world if I could, Charlotte. I hope you know that.'

She frowned because she did not understand him and for a moment he looked as if he might explain, but then he didn't.

Instead he took her hair in his hand and gently pulled her down, rolling on top of her in a single fluid movement.

'I should have met you when I was younger.' His breath was on her cheek, warm and close.

'You did.'

He laughed and kissed her nose and her cheeks and finally her lips. A playful teasing kiss that was different again to all the others he had bestowed upon her.

'How old were you? Then?'

'Fourteen and with all the grandiose ideas of being almost a woman. I wished for years that you might have climbed the stairs and snatched me up from behind the banisters to ride on your white horse to some far-off estate where no one else would have ever found us.'

'I was twenty-five. Full of my own importance. Impatient for life, but I do remember you there.'

'I followed your progress covertly through my brother when he was your apprentice. Afterwards when Silas left your company I still wrote down every scrap of information I ever heard about you and it turned into quite a tome.'

'So that's how you knew of Meghan? I wondered how you realised I would be at the charity Christmas event this year, seeing as I have never attended another before.'

'Well, that was much by chance. Mama mentioned your name because she was supposed to be going, but she cancelled a few weeks ago because she'd accepted an invitation to Lady Alexandra Malverly's instead. I didn't know anything about Verity Alworthy breaking your heart, though.'

He kissed her lips again, this time lingeringly. 'An exaggeration, I think, and the laudanum had a lot to do with my overwrought reaction. Hers was a hand that might have pulled me up from the hole I was in and when she left I thought I should never escape it.'

'But you did.'

'Eventually and through much exertion and when I was better I realised what a lucky escape I had made from both the laudanum and from Verity Chambers.'

He kissed her mouth as he said this, a longer kiss, underscored with the same passion as last night. Not a timid kiss or a gentle one.

Then there was no more talk at all save for the communication between their bodies.

Chapter Thirteen

In the morning she awoke to find him sitting fully dressed in a chair to one side of the bed.

'When you are ready to go home, Charlotte, my driver will take you. I am sorry I cannot accompany you myself, but I have some business to attend to.'

Jasper did not look well. He looked pale and strained and the quiet tone of his voice held none of the life it had in the previous hours.

Had she done something terribly wrong? Was he only now seeing that in their lovemaking some boundary had been crossed and he wished it had not been? The daylight seemed to leach out their secrets, replacing ease with awkwardness and delight with a squalid and shabby truth.

He wanted her gone. He wanted to send her home. Her nakedness beneath the sheets was suddenly difficult given his own full attire and she did not feel like rising before him and parading her wares.

'Can you turn around?'

'Of course.' He looked away towards the window,

an isolated and detached man, the only movement visible the beat of his three middle fingers against the soft arm of his chair.

Counting the seconds until she was no longer there just as they had counted the space between thunder and lightning and the sultry beauty between their kisses.

'Will I see you again, today?' She had to ask because if she didn't she would sit there at the Foundation waiting.

'No. I am afraid not. I shall be occupied for a few days.'

He knew she needed to depart for the country and was expected at the Malverly house party within a few days.

'I see.' These words were dragged from a grief that was rising, but he gave that no matter either. After a few moments when he saw that she was dressed as well as she was able to manage alone he picked up a small silver bell on the table beside him and rang it.

A servant materialised almost immediately.

'I have asked for my carriage to be brought around. Can you find Miss Fairclough's cloak and accompany her to the conveyance please, Larkin? Then see that she is returned safely home.'

'Of course, sir.'

'Thank you.'

He looked at her as he said this and she turned to collect her hairpins still on the bed, slipping the necklace he had given her beneath a pillow, tucked into safety. If he had bequeathed it to her in the throes of passion, he would definitely want it returned in the cold indifference of this morning.

She would take nothing.

She made a point of not looking at him as she passed, her heart shattering as he let her by without saying a word.

He listened to her footsteps, at the door, in the corridor and then down the staircase, small light sounds that took Charlotte from him, inch by inch until there was only silence.

He tried to breathe and find air, tried to sharpen the blur of the room and the growing lack of sound that whirled about him.

His leg howled with pain, twisting into his very centre, a hot core of agony dragging him down into the mire. At least she would not know. At least she was gone. At least when he fell to the floor writhing, she would not see him and she would only imagine him cold-hearted and fickle.

He could fix that when he saw her next. He would even explain about his leg and how the pain made him insulated and solitary. He would say that he did not wish for her to be upset or dismayed and he would go and visit a doctor as soon as he could just in case there was some new treatment that could be tried.

But he could never mend her seeing him as a 'tortured cripple' as Verity once had written. She had happened upon him in the middle of an attack and he had seen the look of horror on her face, the empty hope, the disgust and repulsion and the panic. His

polite and loving fiancée had run from him with all
the haste of one who had seen a demon and perhaps
in that she was not far from wrong.

He never remembered how he acted caught in the
centre of his pain, but he did know that which his butler and his valet had told him. He screamed and swore,
any vestige of being a gentleman long gone under the
influence of his affliction. He hit out when anyone
touched him so that they always left him alone to run
out the worst of it, a feral bestial version of a human,
the blood route in his leg distended and blocked.

This time the renewed and howling discomfort
was uncharacteristically close to the episode of a few
days ago, but he had been making love for hours last
night and the movements had aggravated the injury.

He'd known the moment his groin pained him that
the fragment had shifted. Like the red-hot torture of
a firebrand pulled down his skin until the very form
of his leg began to melt.

He'd left the bed with Charlotte asleep in it and
walked, trying to work out the pain with exertion, trying to loosen the tightness. But nothing had worked
and so he had done the next best thing that he could.

He had dressed himself as well as he was able and
sat, waiting in the chair for her to awaken, keeping
absolutely still because at least in immobility there
was protection.

When she had opened her eyes to find him he'd
seen the softness in her face, the shyness and the
beauty, and his heart broke all over again. He knew
his distance had wounded her. He knew that. He had

left her wondering about his intentions, the priceless gift of her virginity devalued by his apparent apathy.

Swearing, he took in air. He could not fight on two fronts just at the moment, when every part of his being was trying to ward off the pain. He hated the hope of keeping her with him even as he knew that there would be no such choice.

He'd tried to hold her at a distance, tried to tell her that his freedom was important to him.

But Charlotte had crept under his guard, into the soft place inside of him, the place where truth lingered.

He loved her.

He loved her as he had never loved another woman in his life and that was the quandary. He was a cripple with an injury that was worsening and his time was running out.

The doctor he'd seen a few years ago had told him that these episodes would increase in pain and in occurrence and that, apart from severing his leg off entirely, there would be nothing to be done about any of it.

She was twenty-two and beautiful and he should have understood the wrongness of taking all that she had offered him, but he hadn't been able to stop himself.

A short knock on the door had him looking over and Larkin was back, a blanket in hand.

'It's cold this morning, sir. I think this might help.'

'Thank you.'

He waited as the warm wool was tucked in about him.

'Did Miss Fairclough leave?'

'She did, sir, but she asked me to give this to you.'

His butler held out a letter that was folded in on itself, his name in capitals on the outside. Mr King. Not Jasper. When he took the missive he shoved it in his pocket, vowing to look at it only when he was alone.

'Should I call the doctor back, sir?'

'Don't.'

'Your sister, then? Should I let her know…?'

'Absolutely not. If I sleep I will feel better and I will ring for you if I have a need. Under no circumstance are you to let anyone into the house and if Miss Fairclough does return tell her that I have left London for a few days and that I shall call upon her when I am back.'

'I shall, sir.'

'There is one other thing you could do for me before you go. Bring the brandy bottle over with a glass. I am sure I will have a need of it.'

When that was done and the door was shut behind the departing servant, his hand reached into his pocket for the letter.

Unfolding the sheet, he began to read.

No legacy is as rich as honesty.
I hope we can find this between us again.

Not a recrimination, but a gentle reminder of what was important and so like Charlotte that he laid his head back against the soft brown leather and closed his eyes, the prayer that he might have said dying on his lips.

He did not know what to pray for, that was the truth. He did not wish to hurt her again and he could not quite yet chance honesty.

Gripping the small note so hard that his fist began to shake, he got up and dragged himself to the door to lock it.

Lottie arrived home just as the sun rose, the King servant seeing her safe and waiting until the door opened before he tipped his hat and left.

Claire stood there with a deep frown on her face.

'I don't want to hear what you have been doing, Miss Lottie. I don't want to have to lie to your mother and pretend when she returns so we shall say nothing more of this night. We shall simply forget that it has happened and leave for the Malverly Christmas party first thing tomorrow morning when we are packed and well rested. There, in the company of your mama and your sister, you might remember again sense and decorum and a little of the wisdom you used to have before you met Mr King.'

Lottie did not want an argument and after the last half an hour could not have withstood a further emotional outburst, so she nodded and made for the stairs.

'I will help you undress and bathe—'

'No,' she interrupted her maid because she knew that her body was marked with Jasper's lovemaking and she did not wish for Claire to see it. 'I shall simply get into bed and sleep. I have a headache.'

'I see.' The words came quietly, but Lottie was past caring about how she had disappointed yet another person. On reaching her room she simply shut the door behind her, falling back against the wood as she did so and listening to the departing steps of her maid.

Thank goodness she was alone. Thank goodness Mama was not here, nor Amelia. Swallowing back tears, she began to take off her clothes. Her bonnet. Her cloak. Her jacket. Her gown. Her underwear. Her stockings and her boots. They all dropped in a pile around her feet, each layer shedding more in the way of armour and inviting in the guilt.

When she was naked she walked across to her mirror and stood there, bare and small, the red whorls of passion across the white of her skin. This was who she was now. This person. Different from before. Branded. Ruined.

'No.' She shook away that word because even now after being sent from his house she would still not change what had happened. She had known paradise. She had walked the pathways of bliss and given Jasper back as good as she got. Her small smile heartened her. It had not been all one sided, remembering the marks on his back from her nails, her lust imprinted upon him just as visibly as his was on her. Her finger covered one of the whorls at her neck and she tipped back her head, feeling in the movement echoes of her want. Still.

'Jasper.' She whispered his name into the empty space as if she might conjure him. Why had he sent her home? Why had he not accompanied her? Why had he simply sat there looking pale and indifferent and uncaring after such a night? When she yawned she knew she was too tired to think properly now. She needed to sleep. Needed to regroup, the shock of his response dulling the energy she more normally held.

The sheets were welcomed as she crawled into bed, the pillows soft and the dawn light muted. She should wash, she knew that, but she could not find the strength to, the smell of him on her body, his seed inside her. She wondered about that, for he had used protection the first time and then nothing afterwards. Had he simply forgotten?

The thought came that perhaps even now her womb might be cradling the first beginnings of life, though her menses had only just finished. Was it possible she could be pregnant?

Her hands came across her stomach and she held the roundness of it close.

'Please God, let it be.'

A prayer of deliverance and liberation. A child who might be the best of both of them and a way for them to stay together. Surely if he knew there was a baby involved Jasper would behave honourably? He would offer marriage and a home and a future.

Another part of her pushed such thoughts away. A trap to ensnare a man was a poor and inadequate thing that seemed like a wrongness.

Perhaps he thought her wanton? Perhaps most other young woman would not have allowed him the adventure of the sensual, the languid lethargy in the experiment of differing positions, the granted consent no matter what they asked each other. She had been shameless and abandoned and licentious, any chasteness dissipated under the thrall of his touch.

He would have recognised her lack of experience, though, because she had seen the blood between her thighs after the first time and so had he.

God. Her body clenched at that reminder and an ache deep inside her began to throb. Just the thought of him made her impious and a different woman from the one she'd been before. Claire had guessed her secret simply by looking at her.

She tried to imagine what had been so very obvious to her maid. It was not as she might have thought and what she'd overheard her mother and Nanny Beth once say.

'When a girl loses her virginity before marriage there is a sadness in her.'

All Lottie could feel was joy and the hope of more, a secret knowledge that was too new to hide. A treasure.

Her thoughts then returned to the topaz necklace, the stones wrought intricately into tea-rose gold. His mother's? Not an inconsequential gift, then, but one of great value and personal worth.

Nothing made sense. There was no logic in what had just happened.

She would go back to see him this afternoon, to talk, and to try to understand his feelings. She knew hers, after all, and love was much too important to simply throw away on an error or a misconstruction.

On that decision she felt the world around her soften and she yawned, burrowing into the pillows and pulling up the blankets so that she had a cocoon of warmth.

'I love you.' These words accompanied her into the realm of slumber.

Only pain held him now, wrenching him this way and that, the loss of himself more terrible than it had ever been before as he shoved a pillow across his face and screamed into linen and feathers.

The bang on his door infuriated him and made him take in breath, a shaky furious movement that exacerbated the pain and made his leg reel in protest.

'Go…away.'

His valet's voice came quietly through an inch of wood. 'Miss Fairclough insists on seeing you, sir. She says it is important.'

'No…' This was almost groaned.

Oh, please, God, do not let her come…do not let her be there through the door…please do not let her in.

'Sir?'

'Go…away…now.'

This was all he had left as the remnants of sense leaked into unconsciousness. He could feel the pain taking him, leading him to a place that was black and still and quiet. Silence heartened him as he groped for the brandy and swigged it straight from the bottle. Some of it ran from his lips down on to his shirt, soaking the whiteness and staining it. He liked the cold.

Would they break down his door? Could they?

One minute became two and then became five and as the stillness settled he simply let go of it all, the brandy bottle falling to the floor beside him, the shards of glass catching light even as he fell down beside them, a lifeless weight of heat and agony. And finally of darkness.

'Could you tell your master that I shall be back early this evening to try again?'

The servant before her at Jasper's town house looked vaguely frightened, his hands shaking as he opened the door to let her out.

'I should not imagine the master will be back until the morrow, Miss Fairclough.'

A blatant lie. She had heard Jasper's voice shouting, she was sure of it.

'Nevertheless what I have to say is important, so I shall return just after five.'

She did not wait for an answer as she walked away with purpose. She would find a hackney cab as making her own way home today was just too far and she still felt...odd.

She was dislocated by her momentous decisions and by Jasper's strange reactions. He would not just abandon her like this, surely? The horror of everything brought tears to her eyes and she wiped them away.

She would not cry. Not here or now when none of this was her fault and when all she had given him was a gift. This was his problem and his shame. A small coffee shop a street away caught her attention and on a whim she stopped to sit and to buy a hot drink.

She felt exhausted, shaky and sick. She didn't want

to go back home and be scolded again by Claire, her maid's anger having worsened this afternoon by her inadvertent perusal of the markings on Lottie's neck as she had brought in soup after her long nap.

It was three o'clock already and she had told the King servant she would be back at five which was only a few hours away. This time she would insist on seeing his master no matter what he said because she knew he was there. Jasper was hiding out in his bedchamber for some reason, away from everyone.

A glimmer of memory surfaced and she sought to uncover this concealment. He'd sworn at some time in the night when his leg had jarred against hers and from what Lottie remembered it was far more than a small pain. He'd lain there for a moment quietly, the sweat rising and his hand shaking as he had reached for her and drawn her close.

Could he have hurt it badly somehow, so badly that he was now secreting himself away from anyone who might ask after him? Reaching for the cup of coffee she'd purchased, she knew that she was on to something. It would explain things. He was a private and hidden man. Would he imagine himself lessened somehow by such a wound? So lessened that he would lock the door and let no one in?

The coffee helped her, gave her clarity, allowed an intuition that she had lost hold of to gather itself and reconnect. It was the only solution that made sense, the only answer to a conundrum so confusing she had held it to be her fault, her burden, when so clearly it was not.

Well, she would allow it no longer.

With resolve she replaced the empty cup in the saucer and stood, thanking the man in the shop as she left and making towards Arlington Street again.

The same servant as before answered the door and this time she pushed through beside him, standing in the grand entranceway with resolution.

'I think you and I are at an impasse, Larkin.' She remembered his name from the previous evening and used it. 'I know your master in in his room and I wish to see him.'

'He is indisposed, Miss Fairclough.'

Now this was different.

'Indisposed?'

The horror on the servant's face might have made her smile if the situation was not quite so dire, but she was not going to leave here until she understood the truth.

'Mr King does not wish to see anyone at all. He wishes to be left alone.'

'Because of his leg?'

The man before her frowned heavily. 'You know about his leg?'

'I do.' She placed as much directness into her answer as she could. 'Has a doctor been called?'

Lottie could see the will of the servant disintegrating even as she watched him.

'Mr King will not allow it. He insists that any pain will pass.'

She gave him no more time, moving quickly by

him and running up the wide staircase as fast as she could go. Then his bedchamber was in sight, the door firmly closed.

Jasper lay there inert, a shadow in his vision and a lethargy that he had never felt before. This time was the worst his leg had been, the pain more dreadful than he could remember it. Next time he would die, he was sure he would, for he could not imagine surviving such trauma again.

Just when he was getting his life to a point where he might finally be happy, Charlotte's joy and faith translating itself to him in a way that gave him hope, it was all to be snatched away again?

He closed his eyes and tried to find calm, but it seemed so far away he could not claim it. The sudden start of a noise had him refocusing.

'Jasper?'

Her voice. Again. Shaking his head, he tried to understand if what he was hearing was real.

'Jasper. Open the door. Let me in to help you.'

Charlotte! He would not, with the hell of his leg confronting him in every way possible. Dragging himself over to the door, he sat down against it, breathing heavily.

'Jasper?'

Her voice again and close. Was she sitting down on the other side, too, now, merely an inch of wood separating them?

He did not answer, biting down on fury and rage. Which of his servants had let her in? He would fire the culprit when he found out, he swore he would. He would send them packing without any references whatsoever.

'Jasper, please?'

'Leave…me…alone.'

It hurt to talk even, the swollen heat of him cracking under pressure. Bringing his hand up to his eyes, he wiped away tears, a desperation so very palpable he could no longer hold it in. Spilling out. Released into his shame, falling down his cheeks, salt marks on his arm where the runnels dropped next. Just when he had found his heaven, hell had followed. Like before. Before with the laudanum and with Verity.

'No.' He shook his head hard. No, he would not allow that. Charlotte was kind and true and loyal and deserved so much better.

What had the doctor said to him? This could go on for years or you could be dead tomorrow if the shard should pierce the blood lines. What sort of a man did this make him, what sort of a risk? Nobody wanted to live a life with odds like that.

He remembered her soft beauty, her body lustred pearl in candlelight. Closing his eyes, he squeezed them against the recall. Don't think, he said to himself. Don't think, don't think, don't think.

Let her go, let her walk out of his life one step at a time into independence. He could neither leave nor follow. And sure as hell he could not walk along beside her. That was the worst of it. All the dreams he had suddenly been filled with, impossible hopes and desires were crushed under the reality of truth.

'Let me in, Jasper. Let me in to talk.'

More words, rich in entreaty.

Never.

He didn't say it. He didn't have to. His body sweated. An animal. Dying. Barely alive still. He could no longer bend his leg, the engorged distended limb so repulsive to him he wondered how he had not simply perished.

'Let me in. Now.'

Her tone had changed, the soft plea turned to desperation, and he could hear her talking to someone. Then there was the sound of footsteps and orders, orders given without a thought of refusal.

She sounded entirely the Miss Charlotte Fairclough of the Fairclough Foundation on Howick Place, home of good deeds and integrity, the last bolthole of the unfortunate and the underdog and people who had nothing left to lose. The same Miss Fairclough who had never taken no as an answer where suffering was concerned and whose charity was unending and incessant.

He used every ounce of his strength left to bar the door, the pain of movement making him cry out, nausea assailing purpose, weakness replacing hope.

But she had drummed up help and gathered his servants. He heard the small noise of their endeavour roaring in his ears as the door moved, its hinges creaking against the pressure of both the lock and his inert weight. One inch and then two, a crack of light that seared into his head, fresh air and cold. Then the sound of wood tearing, a final breakage.

His hand came up, the self-inflicted bites weeping, crusted blood staining every nail.

'Push again.' Her voice. Sharper now. The dislodging of weight, a further movement, a quiet drag. He scrambled for the protection of a blanket on the floor, trying to lift the wool across him, trying to hide. And failing.

And then she was there, kneeling, tears falling down her cheeks, the smell of lavender and lemon and compassion.

He did not want it.

'Go…away.'

'My God.'

From her such an expletive was surprising, a woman who had never taken the name of her Lord in vain.

He could not look up. He could not find her whisky eyes.

'My God, Jasper.' She repeated this and her hand touched him, there, on the thigh, the cold of her shocking. Like ice scorching his skin.

'You are burning up.'

Ablaze with shame. He did look then and saw neither pity nor embarrassment, neither repulsion nor disgust nor panic.

'I…am…sorry.'

He could not say more as he simply shut his eyes and left her there, gazing down at him in gentleness on the very last moment of his life.

Chapter Fourteen

Was he dead? Her fingers sought a pulse in his neck and found it, thready and shallow, but there.

'Get a doctor. Get him now.' She addressed this to Larkin even while ordering another to bring a mop and fresh hot water with soap and dry towels.

Jasper's servants behind her turned to go, expressions horrified. She was glad they were no longer there and that Jasper had not seen them, had not been exposed to anything more that would hurt him. She pulled a blanket lying on the floor over his nakedness and removed her jacket, fashioning it into a pillow for his head.

Then she stood and opened the windows, letting the cold roll in to dissipate the stench while lighting the scented candle by his bed. After this she collected a bowl of water from the sideboard and, dipping the thick end of a towel in the liquid, she returned to him. The blood around his lips was easily removed as was the sweat from his forehead, hair drenched wet. Her fingers ran through the length, trying to find in tidiness the dignity he needed, trying to reinstate all that he had lost in his aloneness and pain.

He'd been drinking. The remains of a smashed bottle lay on the floor to his left, the shards catching in the candlelight and sending small bursts of light on to his skin.

Every piece of him looked broken, shattered, bent and swollen. There were bites on his hand that broke her heart and the stubble on his chin was dark. A shadow man of night and agony. The scar on his leg looked many times worse than the first time she had seen it. Yesterday? In this bed bathed in moonlight. Could he recover? Was there any way he might weather this and live?

He'd warned her, tried in his way to set her free, allowed her in his moment of need to have the choice. Stay or go. A damaged man. Too damaged?

She shook her head.

'Jasper,' she whispered. 'I will never give up on you, do you hear me? Never. There is nothing you could say or do to make me go.'

He groaned in return and she thought he might have heard her, there in his far-off place of sanctuary. 'I will chase you to your hell and back if need be and you had better get used to it.'

Just for a fleeting moment she thought she saw a smile.

He came to in his bed, the sheets tucked about him in a tight and tidy way. His right hand was bandaged and his mouth was dry.

'Water?'

Swallowing, he tried to say it again, the first attempt a croaky nothing that had not risen above a whisper. But she was there, beside him, sitting in the chair, suddenly awake, her hair escaping its pins and her glance keen.

The beaker was carefully balanced. Not too much and not too little. The lemon flavour stung his cracked lips and he winced.

'Alive?'

She smiled, one hand resting on his chest. He felt the weight of it like a gift. The room had been cleaned, too. There was the scent of ammonia on the edge of air.

'Mr King?' His focus shifted. A man stood there behind Charlotte, a large redheaded man with rosy cheeks and a full beard.

He looked back to Charlotte.

'This is Dr Christopher O'Keefe and he is the doctor at the Foundation. He has had a quick look at your leg already.'

Hope shrivelled. Now she would know how impossible everything was. Now she would know that he had no future whatsoever and that he was a man whom she would be far better off leaving alone.

'Doctor O'Keefe thinks he might be able to help you.'

Jasper felt a smile wind tightly across his mouth. He had heard this before and it had never worked out. A physician who thought he held the answer, until he didn't. A medical wonder that was promised so easily, but did not live up to any expectations.

He wanted to be alone with Charlotte. He wanted to explain and make her realise that it wasn't so simple.

He wished the man might go and she would be here only with him. He reached out his hand and was relieved when she took it.

'Doctor O'Keefe said that he would like to see if he could alleviate your ailment at first light. It would be a quick operation performed under the influence of morphine and he only needs your permission to go ahead.'

'No.'

Her eyes darkened.

'You do not wish to be cured?'

'Not…possible and no…morphine.' He knew he sounded ungrateful, but just at this moment he couldn't withstand another round of empty promises. The very thought of it made him feel sick.

Doctor O'Keefe spoke now, his Irish brogue strong. 'The swelling that has taken place in your leg has dislodged the metal from its previous resting place, I think, and allowed it to linger in a far less complicated position.'

These words lay in line with what he had been told before. The blood routes had been the problem because of their proximity and any stray movement might have ruptured them, death following.

'I think I can feel its edge, you see, because the object has risen in your groin and is nearer to the surface. Is it metal?'

Jasper nodded.

'Are you a haemophiliac?'

'No.'

'Can you move the leg in this direction?'

His hand indicated to the left and Jasper managed this with much more ease than he had during the past few hours. He was in one of his linen nightgowns now and the smell of starch comforted him. The candle by his bed was scented, too, the small plumes of smoke sending up sandalwood and musk.

'I…won't take…morphine.'

He felt Charlotte's hand tighten on his own.

'Mr King was addicted to laudanum once and does not wish to be so again.' Her explanation to the doctor had him swallowing and he saw the man look at him sharply.

Hell, could he have no secrets of his own?

The rain had come again, the splash of it against the window, colder than it had been yesterday. He just wanted to stop and listen to the sound, he wanted Charlotte to stay and the doctor to go, he wanted a drink and a cheroot to dampen down his anxiety. He felt wrung out and exposed and he wanted it to end.

As if the redheaded man realised his thoughts, he tipped his head and made to leave.

'Send word, Miss Lottie, if you need me. I think this could be done without morphine. Perhaps a good shot of liquor might do the same job, Mr King, if that would be more to your liking.'

Jasper did not answer, but merely shut his eyes, tired of the hope and the possibility of something he knew held none at all.

'You can open your eyes now. He is gone.'

Her voice held a tinge of humour within it.

'But he will...be back?'

'That is up to you.'

'Is it?'

Charlotte heard the lingering accusation in his words.

'Christopher O'Keefe is a talented physician. The most talented we have ever had at the Foundation.'

She needed to tell him this, needed him to understand that there was hope in a situation where he so obviously allowed none.

'Happened...before. Others.'

His voice was faint and she knew he was exhausted. The paleness in his face was not as concerning as it had been a few hours back, but the dark rings under his eyes were still most decidedly there.

She would not push him. Not yet. She needed him to find his rest and to let go of his fears. The rain against the windows was soothing and he appeared to be listening to it, a constant and repetitive sound. When his eyes shut she simply waited, not daring to move, and ten minutes later she knew him to be asleep.

She wouldn't stay here tonight. His valet would watch over him and the other servants who were well in force would help. She needed sleep almost as much as Jasper did, a headache forming and her cough freshening again. But tomorrow she would be back to plead the physician's case and vie for the sense of trying something that might help alleviate this agony ever returning.

Laying his left hand down on the sheets, she leaned down to kiss the deep puncture marks across it.

He was safe now.

For this moment there was nothing more that she could do.

Jasper was surprised at how well he felt the next morning. Usually after an episode like the one yesterday he was dragged down and flat for days afterwards, struggling to walk without a stick or even to walk at all.

Today he needed no prop to aid him, the leg much less swollen and discoloured than it had been.

Raising his nightgown, he felt around the area and sure enough there was the edge of the offending metal in a place he had never felt it before. It was also close to the surface and away from the deep blue vein that it had been right under.

Calling for Hutton, he ordered a bath and his clothes. After his toilette had been completed he sat at his desk and ate a hearty breakfast of bacon and eggs and crispy potatoes. It was like an awakening and his gratitude was boundless although he wished Charlotte might return.

He had found her necklace on his desk this morning. His valet had said it was discovered beneath the pillow when he had remade his bed, tucked away in secret.

He could imagine Charlotte doing that when he had almost ordered her gone, her sense of honour unquestionable. She would have left it because of its

personal worth to him, the fact that it was also a priceless heirloom probably barely considered. He did not
know of one other woman of his acquaintance who
would have secreted it away unbidden and never mentioned it again.

He wished she was here. He wished he might ask
her about the doctor and his expertise. A night's good
sleep had opened him to the possibility of having this
piece of metal removed, a hope that was tempting,
especially if the physician could use brandy instead
of morphine to knock him out.

When the doorbell rang an hour later he tensed and
looked at the clock in the corner. He had come down-
stairs to the green salon to wait, wanting to meet her
out of the confines of his bedchamber. The humilia-
tion of her seeing all that he had been made him uncomfortable, but he could change nothing now and
here she was still giving him another chance. The dog
sat beneath his desk. He'd locked it out of his room
when he was struggling with his pain and Hero had
not let him out of his sight since.

When his butler showed her in he stood, the ease
of it gratifying.

'Miss Fairclough.' Far too formal, he knew, but in
the circumstances he stuck to convention.

'Mr King.' There was a lilt in her voice, her gaze
taking all of him in. 'You look so much better this
morning.'

'I could hardly look worse.' These words came
even as he thought not to say them and she laughed.

'Oh, I work at the Foundation and hardship and illness is our stock in trade.'

And therein lay the difference, he thought. She was a woman without guile or deceit, a woman who might tell it as it was without frill or fuss and he liked it. A lot.

The day became brighter and the heaviness of his heart lifted. Suddenly it felt as if he might be able to find the ground he had been upon before she had seen him yesterday afternoon, grovelling on the floor in agony and naked.

The memory of their lovemaking also rose again into the equation because with his strength recovered he could imagine it might happen again and he wanted it to. Desperately.

'I asked Dr O'Keefe to call in on you this morning as well.'

His libido fell sharply on hearing this.

'I have had other physicians telling me of the possibility of success and it has always come to nothing.'

'Doctor O'Keefe is the most talented physician we have ever employed at the Foundation.'

He stayed silent. She'd told him that yesterday, too.

'He reiterated his hopes for a complete cure to your leg. It seems to me you should at least listen to what he has to say.'

'Charlotte.'

The use of her name had her eyes darkening.

'You forgot the necklace I gave you.'

'I thought perhaps that you might not wish for me to have it.'

'After the gift you gave to me the night before last? Hardly.'

A heavy blush covered her cheeks. 'I do not regret the giving of my…gift, either. No matter what happens.'

'Then I am glad.'

And just like that they were back to how they had been, the air between them shimmering with possibility. He reached down and brought the green-velvet box out from a drawer beside him.

'Could I give this to you again?'

When she nodded he stood and she did, too, waiting as she came to him and then fastening the piece around her throat.

'I know it is a bit formal for daywear, but…'

She stopped him. 'It is perfect.'

'And so are you.'

He kissed her carefully and as if he had all the time in the world. He did not hurry or pressure her, he simply gave her himself, without any sort of restraint. He knew she would read an apology into the kiss, but he hoped, too, that she might understand something else.

I love you.

It was too soon to say it perhaps, but he wanted an echo of it, after the hardship and the shame. He wanted her to know of his honesty, lost yesterday in the blackness of pain, but here now, today, after the storm.

The kiss was sweet and measured and truthful. There was lust there, but it was bridled and underneath that was another emotion, one she had not known from him before.

Care, if she might name it, delicate and cautious. When she moved back just a very little she saw that he watched her, his velvet eyes burnished with feeling.

'I thought I may have lost you...' He could not go on.

'I am not a wilting flower, Jasper.'

He laughed at that and she was glad because a tension was broken as well as a wariness that had kept him distant. Now when he leaned forward to kiss her, the edge of it was as sharp as she remembered and as beguiling.

The worry of the last day began to subside and the gold in the topaz necklace warmed her skin. His mother's necklace—she had seen the same piece of jewellery in the portrait on the staircase.

Jasper's mother had his eyes and his colouring, a beautiful woman with a strength in her stance.

'How old was your mother when she died?' Lottie said this as he brought her into his chest, his arms about her.

'The same age as I am now. Thirty-three. My father was never the same afterwards.'

'A hard reality for a child who had just lost a mother.'

When she went to speak again he simply laid his fingers on her lips to stop her and then his head fell lower, across the skin at her throat.

'You are so beautiful, Charlotte. Inside and out.'

She smiled because she wasn't really, but was glad that he thought so.

'I am too tired to do much more today, but could I hold you for a little while?'

She nodded, but came back with an observation of her own as he brought her close.

'You should have told me about your leg, Jasper, instead of trying to deal with it all alone. I could have been there to help you.'

He was quiet for a moment and then he started to speak. 'Verity saw me in the throes of an attack once not even half as bad as this one was and, although I thought she loved me, she sent a note to say that she could never marry a cripple.'

'And you thought that I might think the same?'

She felt his uncertainty like an ache and understood.

'I am not Verity Chambers, Jasper.'

'I know, but—'

She didn't let him finish. 'Would you leave me if I had an injury?'

Her question caught him sideways, the truth in it blinding.

'Of course I wouldn't.'

He felt her take in a breath and when she raised her face to his he saw tears filling her eyes.

'Why not?'

'Because I love you and because there would be nothing that you could do to make me leave you.'

Her chin quivered and more tears came.

'You love me?'

'With all my heart and what is left of my broken body.'

Her fingers around his face held him there. 'Say it again. The love part.'

'I love you, Miss Charlotte Fairclough.'

Her whisky eyes brimmed with joy and wonder and disbelief, all mixed with the tears.

'I love you more than I have ever loved anyone and I always will. Until my very last breath.'

He waited for her to speak, but it appeared that she could not, her emotions too raw and new, and so he simply held her, the firelight playing on the gold and browns of her curls.

After a moment, though, she pulled away.

'My family always said that I am too independent for my own good.'

He waited, not quite sure where she was going with this.

'But when I love, I love for ever, fiercely and protectively, and I do love you, Jasper King, and I have done since I was fourteen years old and my sister danced with you and I was wildly jealous. I have loved you from the moment I saw you through the stair banisters at the Foundation when you came to visit Amelia and I have never loved anyone else. Never. I promise to God that I haven't.'

Her fingers ran across her heart and he caught them, bringing them to his lips, and he was about to say more when a servant knocked and brought through Dr O'Keefe, the doctor looking much more rested this morning than he had seemed last night.

Jasper stepped back from Charlotte and stood still, tipping his head to the newcomer. His timing could not have been worse. He had just proclaimed his love for Charlotte and her own declarations were barely finished. He wanted to take her hand and haul her off into another room to finish such a conversation, alone, but of course he could not.

Charlotte's expression held the same frustration and he was glad of it.

He noticed the doctor had brought a large case with him indicating the tools of his trade. Did he think to elicit a response from him now regarding extracting the metal fragment? God, what if it all went wrong and the blood lines were punctured? He would not have any time to enjoy the love they shared.

Yet if he waited the piece of metal might shift again to a more inaccessible place or a position that was much more dangerous. Or he might have another attack and this last one was the very worst he had ever had by far. Could he survive a further occurrence?

'I hope that Miss Fairclough has talked to you, Mr King, about the small operation that could be performed this morning. It should take no longer than fifteen minutes once you are under the influence of brandy or whisky or whatever liquor you choose. There would only be a little cut and a few stitches.'

A decision? The man was waiting for one, a busy

doctor with other patients to call on and little time to spare.

He looked over at Charlotte and saw in her eyes all the concern that would be in his own and another hundred thoughts ran through his head.

He could not keep on as he had been and he could not expect her to do the same. He wanted a life with Charlotte, one that would be free of the jeopardy he now lived under, but he could not ask her to share such a life if it was all so precarious. He needed to be healthy. He needed to take a chance and live.

'Very well.' The words were wrenched from both fear and hope. 'Where would be the best place to perform the operation?'

'I would need you to be lying down so a bed would be ideal. It would take me about twenty minutes to be ready for you.'

'My chamber is upstairs, then.' He bent down to ring a bell and Larkin came in. 'Please show Dr O'Keefe up to my room. He will be attending to me in the capacity of a doctor so he might need a few things to be provided.'

When the doctor had left he turned to Charlotte.

'Join me in a drink, my love? It seems I have twenty minutes to be completely non-sober.'

Her world spun. Everything had happened so fast. His declaration of love for her, his assent to have the operation and now this. How many glasses constituted enough? She had no idea at all.

Please God, let Christopher O'Keefe be right in his

declaration about the ease of the operation. Please do not let there be complications, for she wanted Jasper for a lifetime and not just one day.

She tried to smile, to find her braveness, but it was a lot harder with so very much at stake.

'He is a very good doctor.'

'You've already told me that. Twice.'

Jasper's voice sounded stronger now that he had made his decision and when he passed her over a glass of what Lottie presumed was brandy she took it gladly. She also needed some fortification.

'I think it will go well, Jasper.'

He was already beginning on his second glass, the first having been downed quickly.

'Well for us both?'

She did not quite understand his meaning as she waited for him to speak. One moment passed and then two.

'I don't want to be a burden. To you.'

'You could never be that.'

He was on his third glass now and his voice was softer, a sense of dislocation heard in the words.

'When it happens…' His hands indicated his leg. 'When this happens…and the pain comes… I think that perhaps it will all stop. Life. And it never mattered before because I did…not have you. Before I almost welcomed it, but now…now I want to live, Charlotte. I do.'

She walked across to him and straight into his arms.

'You will. I promise it.'

He smiled and tipped her head to his.

'I…want…you. I want to make love to you, but…' He swayed and she led him over to a chair and sat him down. 'I want to make love so much that it hurts. Here. And here. And here.' He pointed to his head and his heart and then to his groin. 'But I also…think that right now a kiss will have to do.'

He simply waited as she crouched in front of him and bent to his mouth.

She could taste the brandy on him.

'You are…beautiful, Charlotte.'

More words.

'And lovely and brave and stubborn…and I will take you to Liverpool to see where I work and then… we will go to America. I have never left England because my father was sick for a long time.'

'But you read books of far-off adventure stories? Like the one you gave me?'

'A way…of…escape. Responsibilities held me here.'

He took another swig of the brandy, this time simply lifting the bottle that stood on the table beside him until there was nothing at all left.

'Drunk,' he said. 'Enough,' he added and leant back to close his eyes. 'Once upon a time I was drunk for months. Did I tell you that? Once it was the only thing that saved me. Now it is you, Charlotte. You are my…salvation. I hope I can be yours.'

'You are already.'

'No.' An urgency was back. 'Not like this.' He smiled then and tried to stand. 'If I don't go upstairs soon…might not get there.'

Lottie understood and rang the bell on the table

beside him. A servant she had not seen before came immediately and seemed to know exactly what to do even before she spoke.

She had been waiting here for an hour already and her worry was rising. Jasper had asked for her to go as they had got him into bed.

'Easier,' he drawled as she tried to speak. 'For both of us.'

Two of the King servants had stayed to assist Dr O'Keefe and she had come back to the green salon, her brandy still on the table and barely touched.

She wished Mama might have been here, or Millie, the bravery she had shown Jasper suddenly gone.

If he died…

She shook the thought away and concentrated on the positive. It was a small operation, Dr O'Keefe had said, and he was very certain he could remove the metal fragment without complication.

Complication. The word sat on her tongue like a bitter pill. Jasper believed he could bleed to death if it was touched, he had said as much to her, and some of the doctors before O'Keefe had not been hopeful.

Who was right? Who was wrong?

Please, please help us, she beseeched in a prayer, the reality of a patient dying in what she hoped was a relatively simple procedure suddenly there. She stood and walked to the window. The park opposite was empty, the rain driving everyone away. Further away rooftops could be seen, chimneys smoking to ward off the cold.

In this salon the fire was warm and well stocked. Someone had seen to it while she was upstairs and she was thankful.

She mulled over the words he had said. He had felt the responsibility of looking after his father to be his own? A man of honour and integrity. For how many years had he done that, she thought, and where had his sister been?

A noise from above had her tilting her head, her heart speeding up so much she could feel the beat of it in her throat as she heard footsteps on the staircase.

Then a servant was there a wide smile on his face.

'The doctor said it was a success, Miss Fairclough, and he asked if you would like to come upstairs?'

Within a minute she was in his room. Jasper was asleep and peaceful, the blankets drawn across him and the bed tidy. The dog was asleep on the floor beside him, one wary eye opening as she came in.

'Mr King was the perfect patient,' Dr O'Keefe explained as he caught sight of her. 'He slept through the whole thing with barely a murmur. The brandy he consumed must be one of a good quality.'

'So you managed to extract the metal?'

'I did and with little trouble.'

'So he is…' She couldn't say it.

'On the road to a full recovery,' O'Keefe supplied. 'He is indeed. When he wakes there will be some pain and he will need to favour his right side for a week or two, but other than that…'

Reaching for the large leather bag, he snapped the clasp at the top closed. 'I doubt if he will need to see me again today, Miss Fairclough, though I will call upon him tomorrow just to see that everything is as it ought to be.'

It was almost two hours later that Jasper awoke, his voice strong.

'What is the time?'

'Four in the afternoon. It has just begun to go dark.'

She saw him wriggling his leg, one hand feeling the outline above the blankets just to check that it was still there.

'Doctor O'Keefe said that the operation was a complete success.'

She saw how he swallowed, taking a moment to digest the information.

'He said you might have to favour the leg for a week or two and perhaps use a stick.'

'A small price to pay. Is O'Keefe still here?'

'No. He had other patients to see, but he said to tell you he would be back tomorrow to change the dressing and see how the wound looks. He does not expect any problems.'

He was raising his leg up and down now, amazement written across his face.

'Does it hurt?'

'No, and that is the thing that surprises me. There is no pain whatsoever. Since the accident there has always been pain.'

His voice drew her in, but it held an edge of exhaustion. To jump into the unknown when he had been warned by so many doctors that a cure was not only impossible but also dangerous took real courage. She could hear the consequence of such bravery in his speech.

'You need to sleep, in order to heal. Dr O'Keefe was most insistent upon it.'

He reached his hand over to her and she took it, his fingers entwining through her own.

'I love you, Charlotte.'

And on that pronouncement he fell fast asleep.

Jasper awoke to the birds singing, a state of affairs he had not managed for all the years since his accident. Usually in the night his leg ached so badly he needed to walk out the tension, but now even as he stretched he felt only the small soreness of the cut with its stitches and nothing else.

The operation was a complete success.

He could live his life now without restriction and he had Charlotte by his side to live it with him. She loved him. Had always loved him. With the quickness of this operation he'd barely had time to think about what that meant, to plan for a life together, to let her know that he wanted her by his side until the day they died, hopefully somewhere far into the future.

The dog lay next to him, on the floor, sitting up and stretching when Jasper registered movement above. His hand patted the softness around one brown and white ear and the dog let out a sound of pure delight.

'How is your leg today, Hero?' he asked and ran

his fingers across the wound. A lolling pink tongue came around to stop him, the warm wet of it making him laugh.

'You are like me. We have both been through the wringer, but have come out the other side.'

Pushing back the covers he sat up, his feet against the floor adding no extra hurt at all. Then he stood. The operation site was tender and though he did limp a little on that side it was no more than a dull pain. He did not even reach for his stick at the end of the bed.

He walked then to the windows and back and repeated it. After that he lifted the hem of his nightshirt and saw the bandage was still pristine and unstained. It had not bled or become infected. He thanked O'Keefe beneath his breath with all his heart and Charlotte, too, for bringing such a doctor to him.

The day was still overcast but there were hints of blue in the leaden sky. He would have a wash and get dressed and for the first time in a long while he was truly looking forward to breakfast.

'Are you hungry, boy?'

The dog stood and stretched and tipped its head, a startlingly direct brown gaze trained upon him.

'Let me get changed first and then we will go down and see what the cook can rustle up for us.'

Two hours later Charlotte arrived and was brought through to his library where he sat sorting out the business that needed seeing to. Today she wore the same bonnet he always saw her in, but had on a new dress, one of dark green and gold. For a change the

dress fitted her perfectly and she still wore the necklace of topaz and gold.

She looked like a princess, albeit a shy one, for
her cheeks were flushed and her more usual directness was missing.

'You appear to be back to normal.'

'I am.'

'Nothing hurts?'

'Nothing at all.'

He had made an effort with dressing, because after
the chaos he wanted to look back in charge and as-
sured. Perhaps it was the clothes that had flustered
her, his less-formal garments more familiar.

The dog had risen and walked over to Charlotte,
his tail wagging madly.

'You look much recovered, too,' she said as she
lent to pat him.

'A good night's sleep puts anyone in a better mood.
Hound or man.'

He was different today. The dangerous edge to him
had been softened under the success of the operation
so that she saw more easily both his urbaneness and
the great wealth he had.

He was like no one she had ever met before and
her proclamations of loving him for ever suddenly
felt foolish.

Today he did not take her hand and kiss her palm.
He did not come forward either, but watched her from
a distance, a puzzlement in his eyes. The dog looked
happier to see her than he was.

'Doctor O'Keefe said that he would call in on you later.'

'What is he usually paid for his services?'

A new question, this, and she gave him her answer.

'Cheap for a life then and for a future, do you not think?'

This time there was some humour in his tone and she smiled, liking the way he smiled back at her.

'In the Rookery O'Keefe is called The Miracle Worker. When we managed to secure him as the Foundation doctor we felt blessed.'

'Is being there at the Foundation a calling for you, Charlotte?'

'In some ways it is, but sometimes…' She let that thought slide before beginning again. 'I'd like to see other places, other lands, but I would always want to come home. My father began the Foundation and the work feels too important to simply disregard. Perhaps it is the same with you and engineering?'

'Perhaps, though the job is often in places I no longer wish to be.'

'Where do you want to be, then?' She chanced this question because she could not stand the tension between them a moment longer and because one of them had to take the chance no matter what the outcome.

'In London. Here with you if you will have me.'

At that she walked into his arms and he wrapped himself about her so that she could barely feel the start of him or the end of her.

'I thought…' She stopped.

'What did you think?'

'I thought you might have changed your mind about me given all the future you now have before you.'

'You are that future, Charlotte. It's us from now on.'

His kiss was quiet and soft, a gentle reminder of her place in his life. She was careful not to press in too hard given the fragile state of his leg. A kiss of love in the middle of uncertainty, a way back to him. A promise.

A noise outside had him stepping back and a servant appeared with a note in his hand.

'This has just been delivered, sir, and the man said that it was important that you see it quickly.'

Lottie held her breath. Please do not let it be another chance meeting with Leonard Carvall, for she knew Jasper would want to go and in his condition she knew it would be detrimental to his leg.

After reading the note he handed it across to her, the signature at the bottom that of Mr Twigg.

'Carvall has been run down on the Whitechapel Road and is not expected to make a recovery and Frank Wilkes has disappeared completely.'

'Do you think it was Wilkes who tried to kill Carvall?' she asked Jasper as she finished reading the missive.

'I doubt it. But a man like that must have many enemies.'

'I hope Rosa O'Brian is safe. You said that the laundry was a part of it all.'

'Let's go there now and see.'

'But your leg…?'

'Is fine. You know the advice the doctor gave me. Use your leg carefully, but do not stop walking. The carriage can let us down outside so it will hardly be an effort.'

'And Dr O'Keefe? What if he comes?'

'I will send him a message and ask him to call in later.' One finger brushed down the side of her face as he said this. 'After we have dealt with this, Charlotte, I swear nothing is going to stop us from saying all the things to each other that we need to.'

'You promise?'

'I do.' He leant forward and kissed her nose.

Rosa had garnered her good sense and taken charge of the laundry herself which was in evidence when they got there, two new girls who Lottie had not seen before folding a large pile of clothes.

'They came from Old Pye Street and had no-where else to go so I told them they could work here, for with Wilkes gone and Harriet taking up another job I needed some help. Mr Twigg from the One Tun pub said he would show me how to do the sums and that he would be prepared to put some money into the venture. He was the one who brought the girls here.'

'He also sent a note to Mr King which is part of the reason we came.'

'A God-fearing man he is, Miss Fairclough, un-derneath of the brawn and bluster, and I can tell you that I don't know what I would have done without him. Mr Carvall is very poorly and it is whispered some of the establishments in the Irish Rookery are not expecting him to come back at all.'

'Probably a blessing.' Jasper's words were harsh.

'Mr Twigg said he has some business with you that he needs to discuss. He should be here shortly.'

Lottie was relieved Carvall would no longer be threatening them, though with her experience in the Rookery she also knew that when one man fell another of his ilk rose.

It seemed that Jasper was having exactly the same thoughts for when Twigg arrived a few moments later he came straight to the point.

'Do you think Leonard Carvall was deliberately hit?'

The big man frowned. 'By a partner of Carvall's, you mean, sir? It might behove you to be watching those girls who you place in the laundry then, Miss Fairclough, though I have promised Mrs O'Brian that I will be looking out for her.'

'What of Wilkes?' Jasper wasn't finished with his questions.

'Frank Wilkes would have been under Carvall's protection and he ran at the first sight of trouble. To the north, would be my guess. Liverpool. Manchester. Other big places to start again.'

'If Wilkes did indeed run, Mr Twigg, then I think it is safe to say that there must be other threats.'

'To the laundry?'

Jasper's voice was quiet as he answered, 'I would not be surprised.'

'I'll be mindful then, sir, and don't you worry, Miss Fairclough, for I will watch over the girls in our care.'

Half an hour later as they made their way home to the Foundation, Lottie was uncertain.

'You think there will be more trouble, then?'

'Perhaps not for a while, but eventually they will be back, the secret ones who have much to gain from this enterprise.'

'The ones who had Carvall nearly killed?'

'The thing you learn about the underbelly of the criminal world is that there is always a tiered system of control. Carvall may be gone, and Wilkes with him, but you can be sure that the ones further up will still have a hand in it.'

'You sound as though you have experience in this world?'

'The opium dens have their own masters and at one time I was well aware of them. My advice would be that the Fairclough Foundation watches those who they place in the laundry carefully, though Rosa O'Brian and Twigg's presence there will be a deterrent.'

'I shall tell Mama that when I see her next.'

'When will that be?' His tone was different now.

'I have to be there by Christmas.'

'Don't go yet then, Charlotte. Stay here with me.'

It was the last word that did it, a tremor in the entreaty that wore down any resistance. They needed to resolve things between them one way or another and already she could feel her desperate need for him building. Now that his leg was dealt with and the prostitution ring that had harboured Harriet White had been broken there was nothing in the way to drag them apart.

In that there was both a freedom and a binding, and yet with no true promise to the other there was also an inherent danger.

Should she keep up this liaison which was precarious in a society that forbade premarital sex? Precarious to her reputation and to her personally, for they had not used any form of control in their last couplings and Lottie was savvy enough to know the risk in that.

She knew that she should return to the Foundation and have him call on her there, a proper courtship observing the rules of an engagement of the romantic kind.

So far sex and lust had taken precedence, the bursting impatience of knowing each other's bodies being their priority. Granted, they had declared their love for each other, but Jasper had not taken that further, a combination of lack of time and unusual circumstance counting against them.

Her mother would have been horrified to learn of her decision to go to the bed of Jasper, but suddenly Lottie could not care. She wanted him again in any way that she could and to be at this moment lying with him in the sunshine in the middle of the day. Nothing else mattered but them.

'Yes. I will stay with you.'

He smiled and took her hand, carefully, quietly,

a warmth that held her captive until they were once again at the King town house on Arlington Street.

Jasper closed the door behind them as they entered his room, the light slanting across the bed. All he could imagine was her limbs bathed in warmth and naked under this new day.

God, she was like a witch, full of magic and power, her smile all-knowing and sensual.

'I want you, Charlotte.'

'I know.'

'Now.'

He lifted her then and laid her on his bed, pulling up her skirts and unlacing the fall of his pants. No preamble, no quiet overture, but the racing honesty of a man at the very end of his patience.

When he entered her she breathed in, opening her legs and calling him home. The bandage on his thigh was wide and thick, but it did not hinder him at all as he pressed in, the sun warming them both and pleasure rising to a crescendo and beaching upon them in waves of glory.

When he lay down across her she waited, their hearts drumming and the noises of the day outside coming back into the room.

'Marry me, Charlotte.'

He whispered these words, no hesitation in them.

'Marry me and give me children and stay with me for all of our lives, for I cannot live without you. I swear it.'

He knew he should have said these words on a

bended knee with a ring in hand, but after the throes of a passion that had brought them back into oneness he could not wait.

He pulled back, but not yet away, a joining still there.

'Yes,' she whispered, a happiness in her words that made his heart swell. 'Yes, I will marry you, Jasper King, and give you as many children as you desire.'

'Let's start with this one, then,' he returned, taking her hands in his own and raising them above her head.

This was a language between them that was unspoken, but every nuance of movement echoed intent and commitment as he simply looked at her and told her everything.

'In the dens of morphine and laudanum I imagined I would never escape. I thought I was to be trapped there, in the iniquity and in the stupor. I thought the taste of bitter almonds and strong alcohol was my only home, a place of purgatory, a place of despair. There were things that happened there...'

He stopped and she waited, the gold in her eyes brittle.

'Things I am not proud of. Shameful things. Things that rose in the clouds of smoke and inertness, things I cannot describe.'

'Then don't. You told Harriet not to look back. You told her to take one breath and live, to take one step and live. You told her that and she believed it. Now you have to do the same, Jasper. You have to forget. You are a good man, an honourable man, a man who would save a young woman he had never met despite all the dangers faced, a man who would look after his father when he was ill and despite any difficulty, a man who would watch over his sister with love. A steadfast man. A man of principle. A man I love.'

'Charlotte?' He took her hand in his, the smallness of it belying all her strength. 'Let me show you just how very much I love you back.'

Afterwards Lottie lay there, spent and quiet, the last tremors of desire weakening and a new understanding dawning.

'I hope I did not hurt your leg.'

He laughed at that and rolled over. 'Ecstasy and obsession far outweigh pain, my love, and I would take them any day.'

His finger trailed across her stomach, all her clothes removed now. She felt her skin draw in at his touch.

'I will buy you a ring of topaz to match your eyes with stones of gold and amber and translucence.'

She smiled. 'I never felt beautiful, Jasper, until I met you.'

'Then I am glad for it, otherwise you may have been snatched up by another with your whisky eyes and your curling hair of every shade of brown.' His hands ran over her hips and her breasts. 'And that is not even accounting for your curves, soft and full and mine.'

His mouth dipped to one nipple, his tongue running around the shape. When he looked back up, his eyes were dancing in humour.

'Once upon a time Cinderella met Prince Charming,' she said, 'but had to wait for years and years until she grew up before he saw her.' Her voice sounded unlike her own.

'Oh, but I did see you, Charlotte, in my dreams and now right here in my bed, and very soon I shall take you in my carriage to the Malverly country party to ask your mother for the blessing of your hand in marriage.'

'Mama will love you as I do, with her whole heart.'

'We will tell Meghan before we go as well for she has often despaired of me ever finding the perfect wife. After we are married we will go to America and other far-off places, places I have read about on the other side of the world. Then we will come home to London and begin to make a host of children all with curly hair and whisky eyes and bravery and stubbornness and compassion.'

'Jasper?'

She waited until he looked up.

'I will love you for ever and ever.'

'Like in the fairy tale?' His eyes were light.

'No, even better.'

When he kissed her, her arms came around his neck and Lottie knew that she was in exactly the place that she was meant to be, her Prince Charming beside her, a whole world and many years before them.

'Thank you, Nanny Beth,' she whispered beneath her breath, the infinite possibilities of life now a reality and a future she could never have dreamed of stretching out. Sometimes dreams did actually come true. She knew that they did because she held one close, right here in her arms.

* * * * *

*If you enjoyed this story,
look out for the next books in the
Secrets of a Victorian Household miniseries*

Miss Amelia's Mistletoe Marquess
by Jenni Fletcher
Mr Fairclough's Inherited Bride
by Georgie Lee
Lilian and the Irresistible Duke
by Virginia Heath

*And in the meantime, check out
Sophia James's
Gentlemen of Honor miniseries,
starting with*

A Night of Secret Surrender